EliteRoyalties LLC Publications

CHRONICLES OF

"CRUSH ONYX"

A NOVEL BY:

Geoffrey McClanahan

Published by EliteRoyalties LLC Publications

PUBLISHER'S NOTE:

This book is a work of fiction. Names, Characters, Places, and incidents either are products of the author's imagination or are used fictitiously. Any resemblance to actual events or locales or persons, living or dead, is pure and entirely coincidental.

Author: Geoffrey McClanahan

Cover Design: Brand Concepts Creative Media

Interior Format: Write On Promotion

CHRONICLES OF
"CRUSH ONYX"

CHAPTER ONE:

"CRUSH IT GOOD"

First name Crush, last name Onyx, sits on the balcony to her condo located at Central Park west. One million, four hundred thousand spent, was like buying a ten cent box of lemon heads. Being her condo was one floor below the pent house view; crush could still see clearly all the action and beauty Central Park can offer a person whom has recently moved to the Big Apple. Although Crush has been there a few years now, it's always still new and exciting to her. Looking through the double French doors, custom made to her liking, Crush takes a short breath. Scanning her sunken in living room, with custom made Heather Victorian furniture, she places the tip of her pointer finger on the bottom of her lip and begins to nibble on the chipped nail polish. Just staring into space. Eyes wide open, and Paused.

"Come on Crush! Let's not start this bullshit again. I swear to God, if I wasn't stuck inside this brain of yours, I would have put a bullet inside you myself. Such a fucking----"

"You know what Onyx? I don't care for you either. But being you have no more control; and I mean, NO FUCKING CONTROL over me, let's just sit here and enjoy what we, I mean, what I have accomplished. Or maybe you prefer going back into your lonely room?"

"You see what I'm saying Crush! That damn Dr. Korvach got you so fucked up, we can't even argue without you getting on some threatening to put me in the lonely room bullshit! You need to check yourself bitch! Remember he's the reason why I'm here in the first place. But then again, we were born into the same brain and body. But that's not the fucking point. It's too bad you had to go and kill a good piece of Dr. Dick."

"SHUT UP ONYX! JUST SHUT THE HELL UP! I swear, one more dumb sentence that comes out your-----.

"Say it Crush. What, my mouth? I don't have a mouth Crush. It's just me stuck here inside your head!"

Onyx begins to sing a classic song from the Singer and Artist known as Prince.

"You need another lover, like you need a hole in your head, baby baby."

"Ok Onyx, time for you to go. I'll let you out when you're ready to act correct."

"Whatever Crush......"

Before Crush closed Onyx in the lonely room located in the far part of her psyche, Onyx managed to squeeze out a *"fuck you"* as the voice faded away. Crush rolled her eyes and sucked her teeth in disgust.

Crush glanced back into the living room where she had placed her purse on the far corner of the couch. She thought for a moment, pondering on whether or not to take the prescribed medications to calm herself down. Crush waved her hand in the direction of her purse and mumbled, "Forget that crap!" she grabbed her favorite evening drink, a cold bottle of bubbly Dom Perignon champagne. One day short from the first day of summer, Crush let the warm air intertwine through her long silk medium champagne colored hair. She rubbed a piece of ice onto the nape of her neck from the bucket. The water melted from her body heat and flowed down between her perfect breast, and down to her belly button. The drops of water collected to create a small puddle in the middle.

Crush was perfect in every aspect. Her body was flawless. She was very discreet in her personality, but having Onyx around to add excitement, she would let go once in a while. So she laid there on the patio chair in a two piece thong set. Body parts everywhere. The sun started to beat down on her body. Crush took a sip from her champagne glass, put it down, and grabbed her Channel frames. She put them on her eyes and decided to catch a quick snooze. In the process of doing so, she began to watch the streets while New Yorkers did their normal shuffle. Although the city streets are narrow in width, central park provides miles of space to have fun and enjoy the day in the sun. It never stopped the young girls from playing their girly games that had no racial barriers to cross. White, black, Indian, or whatever the ethnic background is, girls will just be girls. Such as playing jump rope, or just being a teenage girl braiding her boyfriend's hair on the bench. Boys jogging by hooting at the pretty girls as they run by or just sitting down next to an elderly couple watching the way they still love each other. Even after all of those years aging together, they let nothing like time separate their bond. Crush put a smile on her face and began to laugh out loud remembering all the little girly things she used to do on the large dairy farm as a child in Madison County, Iowa. That was before the episodes began between her and her split personality Onyx, causing society to give her full birth name separate identities as individuals. Even though there was only one body attached to the birth name, just split her full name in half CRUSH ONYX

Falling into a comatose sleep for a few hours Crush was awoken by the sound of her cellular phone buzzing from the patio table. She leaned up rubbing her sleepy eyes and noticed the name displaying on the caller ID box. The name read Tracy Campbell. Tracy worked at a beauty salon and spa located in Harlem. Crush had forgotten about her 5 pm appointment to get a facial and a quick one hour body massage. She looked at the time on her diamond beveled Blvgari watch. The time was 5:45 pm. She reached over and answered in a sweet girly voice.

"Oh My God! Tracy, I'm so sorry sweetie. I closed my eyes for a few minutes to unwind and that was the end of that shit girl. I fell out."

"Come on Crush. I am not even tripping. You are one of my best clients, girl." Tracy gave the same sister-girly voice in return.

Tracy was in her mid thirties, about 5'5", with a short hair cut. She called it the Halle Berry in Harlem cut. She was very petite, bronze skinned and had light hazel eyes. She used them to her advantage when it came to scooping up a fine brother.

"Listen Crush! I have this big old babbling bitch all up in my ear screaming about, why should she have to wait if my 5:00 pm is not here and shit? You know I'm not even trying to rub that football line backer's back for an hour. So please just tell me you're on your way girl?"

"Oh shit are you serious Tracy? Is she really that fucking big?" Crush began to laugh out loud over the phone.

"Crush I'm dead ass serious! Our policy is one hour after a no show; move on to the next available client. So that gives you fifteen minutes to get your ass over here."

Crush could hear the plus sized woman's voice in the background giving the owner an ear full of complaints.

"Ok Tracy, I'm on my way. I'll be there in ten minutes. So breathe easy my sister. I'm on my way."

Crush hopped up with a great big smile on her face. Tracy was the first person she met from New York City. Crush had met Tracy three years back on a cruise vacation she took, that was suggested by her previous therapist, after the mysterious death of her first and only therapist since birth, Dr. Kenneth Korvach. Dr. Korvach was ranked top in his field for the study of multiple personality disorders, and first to successfully separate the alter ego in the human psyche.

During Crush's two week stay at the "Viva Wyndam Fortuna Beach Resort" Grand Bahamas Island, Bahamas, Tracy was also enjoying a hard earned vacation. Both separate, not knowing each other yet, they both were looking to get their freak on. Tracy and Crush introduced themselves to each other at one of the island's hotel bars over a few drinks giggling and laughing at all the corny men talking their tired ass game trying to get into their panties. Most of them were rich, old businessmen, or young drug dealers flossing and spending cash. Crush was approached by a famous rapper and was asked to join him for a few drinks and hang out with his road crew. He even promised to put her in one of his next rap videos. Crush was already wealthy with hundreds of millions from her parent's trust fund inheritance. So, that wasn't impressive to her at all. Plus, she was no fucking groupie falling all over the celebrity status of a rapper. She declined politely, and just decided to sit and get to know her new friend a little better over more drinks.

Being one week into their vacation, and no decent dick available, Crush and Tracy found themselves having their first bisexual experience together one night. Even though it was for one night, and they both agreed that they were never into woman, they enjoyed the experience and became close friends in the end.

Crush ran to her room in a frenzy looking for something to wear. She opened the top draw to her oak wood dresser and snatched out a pair of Seven low riders jeans that hugged her ass real nice. She then hustled over to her huge glass doors that lead into her walk-in closet. She pulled an Indian print smock top off the hanger and topped her head with an orange colored straw fedora hat.

She rolled over her king size bed, bouncing off the edge back to her dresser at the same time putting on the smock neck blouse. She then wrapped her long hair up in a bun. After putting on the fedora hat pushing it to the front, she grabbed a matching pair of orange leaf earrings out from her large jewelry box, and a gold beaded necklace with emerald drops. Topping off her cutesy outfit, she reached under her bed and pulled a pair of open-toed Dolce & Gabbana sandals and slipped her feet into them.

She checked herself out in the large mirrors that were on the slide open closet doors. Rushing back into the living room she placed her cellular phone in a large off white leather Dolce & Gabbana traveling bag that she used as a purse. Giving a quick scan of her condo, she rushed to the door grabbing the keys off the key hook on the wall.

Getting on the elevator, Crush put the key in a slot that read "parking". Fiddling around in her bag she forgot how fast the elevator reached the bottom level to the underground parking lot belonging to the condo complex. There were three tenants waiting for her to exit out. They said hello to Crush as she smiled and greeted them back in return. Even though the sun was still beaming down on New York City at a quarter to 6 pm, the dim lighting underground still gave a gloomy feel to the atmosphere around every corner Crush turned. Walking in a fast pace turning the corner to go down the ramp to where her cars were parked, she decided to drive her newest baby, the platinum Ferrari Scaglietti 612, with F-22x 9 Spielio-6 customs painted black on chrome rims. Parked beside that was her big boy, a black Hummer H2 with 28 x 10 big homie 8 chrome rims and dark tint.

Reaching in her bag to retrieve the keys, she was startled by a man leaning against the spare tire on the back door of the Hummer. He was about 6'4", light skinned, with a low Caesar hair cut, clean shaved face, smoother than a baby's ass with slanted piercing eyes. The handsome man was wearing a two button peak lapel suit by Lanvin Paris, a pink cotton button up shirt, square tipped Kenneth Cole shoes, a Cartier watch with no diamonds and a black leather band, showed that this man was about his money. Not your street type hustler's feel...more business than flossy. Standing there with both his hands in his pockets gave Crush an uncomfortable feeling inside. She could not remember knowing this man from the present or the past. The silence was thick for a few seconds before she spoke...

"Oh my God, you scared me!" Crush said with her girly voice.

The handsome black man took two steps in her direction with both hands in his pockets.

"You really have no idea who I am? Do you?" he said with one eyebrow up and a small sinister smirk on his face.

Crush took one step back and clinched her purse closer to her chest. She also noticed his eyes were directed towards her breast as he was making his comment.

"I'm sorry but, no I don't know who you are and if you don't mind, I really would like to get to my car please. Thank you."

The man ignored her reply and took another step closer with that stupid smirk on his face.

"I'm only following your orders as you requested madam, Five years to this day, minute and hour. I have to say this is almost uncanny. Those cloths you're wearing? That voice you have? It's bananas."

The man started to laugh out loud as if he knew something she didn't. Only something Onyx would know. Something Onyx had planned with her sick and twisted ways. Crush could do only one thing. Stand there with a puzzled look on her face.

"You-you know Onyx?" she asked with her eyes wide open.

"Yes I know Onyx! I know Onyx inside and out. If you know what I mean, but meeting you Crush, it's like double the pleasure."

Crush was offended. In fact, she was disgusted by that. The man reached inside his jacket and pulled out his mobile phone. He flipped it open and pressed the speaker button telling someone it was time. In seconds she heard the screeching of tires. The eco was loud. She stood there and watched a black GT Bentley hug the corner turning down the ramp towards both of them. The Bentley came to a slow crawl and then a complete stop right in front of Crush. She looked very angry clinching her purse even harder.

She watches the tall handsome man whistle and walk towards the passenger side door. As he looked back at Crush, he gave a sexual licking of his bottom lip in her direction. He opens the car door hopped inside slamming the car door behind him.

Just when she thought the car would pull off, the driver's door flung open and the passenger side window went down. Out of the driver's side door, a young petite girl hopped out. She couldn't be no more than nineteen years old. She watched the young girl walk to the hood of the car, fold her arms, and planted her perfectly shaped hips against the Bentley hood. With a slight scratchy but girly voice, she said out loud to someone in the passenger door window....

"We traveled too far, and waited too long to miss this moment Leto!"

"You are so right Asteria!" the voice answered back as yet another young petite built black girl stepped out from the passenger door.

Crush found herself staring at two teenagers who were identical twins. Yet she could see the difference in their features. Being it was also the middle of June, Crush noticed all the black being worn by the two girls. The tall handsome man sat in the back seat silent. Crush looked at both of them, up and down, and couldn't help to admire their taste in clothing. To be so young their clothes said CASH! They also were dressed in the same outfits as well. Like a mother would dress a set of identical twins. Eyes: over sized glasses by Gucci. Ears: brook earrings of gold and Austrian crystal. Neck: Onyx necklace by Dorian Webb. Body: They both had on one piece Capri length cat suits by Gucci. On their arms hung Claudia Hobo leather handbags by Kooba from one of those Saks Fifth Avenue stores. On their wrists they had matching wooden bangles with 14K gold grommets.

What caught Crushes eye the most was what was on their fingers. They were wearing something that looked familiar. Something she could remember from her childhood life, a very important memory, it reminded her of her mother. It was the Cabochon ring of onyx and 18K gold trimmings that wrapped around their middle fingers. She continued to look at the gold grommet Gucci leather belts and black stiletto open toed Gucci sandals. These girls were dressed up something serious. Their hair texture was as soft and silky as her own.

As they began to talk, it sounded weird to Crush, because every spoken sentence seemed to be split between them both. Standing there in awe, Crush begins to back up towards the driver's door to her Ferrari. As she fumbles with her car keys trying to put the key in the door frantically, she drops them and kicks them under the front tire.

Asteria begins to speak, "How rude of us—
Leto: "not to introduce ourselves--"

Asteria." to you-."

"I'm Asteria Onyx!"

"And I'm Leto Onyx!"

Asteria, "But we're here for our MOTHER!!"

Leto, "The woman locked in your head!!"

Crush's eyes began to fill up with water, mostly out of fear. She could not believe what was being said. How? How was it possible to live for thirty-seven years and not remember giving birth to children? She began to think to herself, while tears rolled heavy down her cheeks. "Dr. Korvach? What have you done?" She dropped down to her knees and landed leaning against the fender of her car.

The back window to the Bentley rolled down as the pretty faced man shouted.

"Okay Asteria and Leto! That's enough! Your mother's instructions are still to be followed! Now let's go! My pretty and deadly TWIN ASSASSINS!"

Asteria smiled at Crush and mumbled. "Look at her, fucking pathetic!"

Leto also smiled at Crush and said in a sarcastic child's voice…"Don't worry mummzie wummzie," then Asteria joined in unison. "We'll be right here when you get back!" Laughing out loud, as Asteria and Leto, the "Twin Assassins", turned away getting back into the Bentley. Crush could see two nickel plated 390 automatic hand guns neatly placed in the small of their backs tucked under their belts.

Her eyes began to blink rapidly as they drove off, up and out of the underground parking lot. Crush fell into a deep shock!

CHAPTER TWO:

"OPENING DOORS"

The family driving a four door 750 LI BMW, bone white, pulled into their parking space directly across from where Crush was still in awe on her knees. Looking out the back window of the BMW, two blond, blue eyed boys were playing with two plastic superhero dolls when they noticed Crush sitting on the ground with her face frozen in a scared fixture. They started to scream at their parents across their seats. "MOMMY, DADDY! There's a lady on the floor!" As the mother turned her head, about to slap them in their faces for screaming so damn loud, she looked through her side view mirror and realized that, in fact, there was a woman sitting on the floor.

"Honey there's that new tenant who moved in a few months ago. She's......just.....sitting there...on the ground!"

"Really sweetie, are you serious?" The husband replied back as he also looked into her side view mirror.

The woman grabbed her purse and opens her door frantically as she instructed her kids and husband to sit still while she investigated the situation. The two little boys began to act like spoiled brats screaming at the top of their lungs. "MOMMY I WANT TO SEE TOO!" only to be muffled by the slamming of her door. Walking toward Crush, the woman looked in both directions up the ramp way, and then down to the next level in a paranoid motion hoping no one was there to do her any harm, or if someone was hiding in the shadows preparing to spring out and attack.

Feeling relieved to know she was safe, she kneeled down and asked Crush what her name was. She repeated to ask several times before realizing Crush was in some sort of shock. She kindly told Crush that she was calling for help also brushing the loose hanging hair from across Crush's face. She reached inside her purse shuffling items around to get to her cellular phone. Thinking out loud she stated, "How am I going to get service two levels down?" She noticed another car making its way down the ramp. She stood up flagging the car to stop. The driver floored the brakes coming to a screeching full stop. The woman saw the angry reaction on the driver's face through the windshield as she trotted towards the car in front of her. The angry black woman in the driver's seat flung the car door open taking her earrings off, as if she was about to open up a can of whip ass on the stupid white chic who jumped in her path.

"WHAT THE FUCK IS YOUR PROBLEM! Are you fucking crazy lady!?"

"There's a woman over there that needs some medical assistance. Someone has to go outside and call 911?" the woman said in a calm voice hoping not to get her ass kicked by the angry black woman.
"What woman?"

"The young woman by that Ferrari!"

The angry sister sucked her teeth in disgust as she and the blond woman walked over to the Ferrari.

"OH MY GOD!! It's Crush!"

The woman whom appeared to be angry at first was now filled with concern. The angry woman in fact was...Tracy! She was on her way to Crush's apartment to leave a note for her at the front desk with the doorman. The note was about leaving her there at the salon with that big fat woman.

Tracy began to act so frantic and hyper, she shoved the keys to her Mercedes Benz in the blonde woman's hand pushing her to go outside and get an ambulance. The blond handed Tracy her keys back, ran frantically back to her BMW, and told Tracy she would bring back the medical assistance and to watch over her friend.

One hour later, Tracy sits patiently on a hard blue chair cramped in between a parent and her screaming infant, and a young thug with blood stains on his white T-shit and Timberland boots in the Waiting area at Mount Sinai Hospital located in mid town Manhattan. The noise was thick. She begins to shift from side to side trying to remain as patient as she can. Holding on to Crush's personal belongings, the ringing of Crush's phone draws Tracy's attention to the Dolce Gabbana bag. Crush was stripped down bare ass for a physical examination to determine what was wrong, or if her body suffered any physical damage. Tracy scrimmaged through Crush's items to get to the phone. Finally reaching the phone and pulling it out, she saw the name Brian in the caller ID box. Tracy remembered Crush talking about her boyfriend Brian Century. Brian was Crush's first boyfriend from her home State Iowa. Brian Century was from Henry County, Iowa. They became good friends during Crush's teenage years at the "Institute for Mental Disorders Research Estates" founded by Dr. Kenneth Korvach in the early 60's. They built a sexual relationship thereafter for many years to come. All the way up until present day

Tracy pressed the talk button and introduced herself to Brian.

"Hi Brian, this is Tracy. I'm Crush's best friend here in New York. I'm sitting at the hospital with Crush now."

"Yes, Tracy I heard a lot about you. Is she ok? Is everything going to be alright? What's going on over there?" Brian sounding very concerned.

"I'm not sure Brian? I mean one minute she was on her way to get her hair done, and then the next strangest thing happened? She...she went into some sort of SHOCK?"

"SHOCK? What kind of shock? The kind of shock like if someone was to lose a limb, a leg, or an eye kind of shock?"

"No Brian. Not that serious, really, really weird. Like if she saw a man get his head chopped off shock? Her face looked like she saw a ghost. It was really creepy but physically, she's fine."

"This shit sounds crazy". Brian mumbled. "Ok Tracy I'm getting on the next available flight to New York. Find out the doctors name and call me back ASAP. I'll see you in a couple of hours."

"Ok Brian. I'll find out how long they plan on keeping her here at the Hospital. After that, I will go stop by her place and grab some personal items. You know...some girl stuff."

They both began to chuckle over the phone receiver hoping it would calm down the intensity in the atmosphere. Brian hangs up on the other end. Tracy puts a smile on her face and hangs up as well. She starts to think to herself as she walks in the direction of the nurse's desk whether Crush had mentioned to Brian about them eating each other's pussies out on that vacation trip were they met for the first time. If so, how will she feel meeting him in person now that he might know their deep secret? Even if it was suppose to be a hidden and never tell endeavor.

Meanwhile in Room 302, Crush is on the hospital bed eyes wide open with both arms by her side. She was covered up to her breast with a soft white blanket while both Dr. Karen Sanchez and Dr. Thomas Thorp were bouncing theories around as to why Crush was in shock. The beautiful Dr. Karen Sanchez was Hispanic, with a perfect body and jet black long hair tied up in a pony tail that still reached the arch of her ass. She walks back over to the EKG machine with a clip board in one hand, and pen in other. Karen taps the pen against her oval round Gucci frames. She shakes her head back and forth while reading the squiggly lines beeping on the EKG machines display monitor. Dr. Thomas Thorp scratches his bald and pale scalp staring at Crush while twiddling a little pocket sized flash light around in his right hand. He then walks over to the bed where Crush lays limp with a motionless expression still on her face. He shines the light directly into her left eye.

"Karen? It would be one thing if her eyes were dilated. If so, notice how her eye gives no response to the light? Even if a person is unconscious, the pupil should react away from the light."

"I know Tom. It's like she's not even alive…mentally that is. Her heart rate and pulse are at normal readings too. During any kind of stress to the system, she should be reading above normal until we give her a sedative to calm her down. But we can't do that with these readings. It would cause a reverse reaction and that would be grounds for malpractice."

"Karen thanks for reminding me to be in court for you next time you decide to snitch." He said as he nudged her shoulder.

"Seriously Tom, where is she in there? It's like she's dreaming with her eyes open?"

"Obviously we have a rare and unique young lady to deal with Karen. Maybe we should call Dr. House or the crew from Fringe. Ok seriously, let's find out as much information about who she is and get some medical background. There's got to be some records in the system about-----."

Before Dr. Thorp can finish his sentence, Crush reached out rapidly grabbing his arm tightly pulling him roughly to her side. He dropped the light and grabbed Crush's hand to release the tight grip she had on his arm. As Dr. Sanchez rushed to aid him, Crush released his arm slowly looking straight up into his eyes, gave him a chill as her eye lids fluttered then closed shut for a few seconds. The EKG machine went hay wire showing massive stress levels.

"WHOA!" Dr. Sanchez mumbled. Thorp looked a bit puzzled. They both giggled in unison for a few seconds. Then Dr. Sanchez placed Crush's arm back to her side.

"If you mention a word about how scared I looked Karen, I'll kill you!" replied Dr. Thorp.

"Well that's more like it anyway Tom. She was starting to freak me out. She's stable now. So how about we go out and get some coffee. Then we can go over her records."

Walking out of Room 302, both Dr. Sanchez and Thorp were approached by Tracy with pen and pad in hand asking questions about Crush's condition. The door closing to the sound proof hospital room and gave the most silent and still feel to the dim area surrounding Crush's hospital bed. Neutrons and electrons began to explode like fireworks in Chinatown during "The Year of the Dragon" celebration in Crush's head. Visions of her past experiences fought on the battle field of her cerebellum cortex. Being in a dream state, Crush could feel her soul being pulled through doors leading her to a past she believed she had once lived. Voices echoed in and out her eardrums as her soul traveled through spotted visions of a place she once loved so much. HOME!

Knowing she was still dreaming, Crush opened her eyes to find herself standing in an open field filled with green grass and bare foot.

Her hair was in two pony-tails with white ribbons on both ends. She was wearing her favorite silk blue, with orange and purple polka-dot scarf flapping in the soft warm breeze. She had on an orange tank-top that came up and over her belly button and her favorite white cotton summer dress that hugged her teenage growing hips. Crush spun around with a great big smile on her face as she recognized all the hills and planes that surrounded the valley, the Redwood trees at the top, with red-necked pheasants she would chase and try to catch when she was a bit younger then that moment. The pollen was so thick in the air; she would have to brush it all away with a swipe from her hand. The beautiful large butterflies that would circle her as she danced in the field joyfully before it was time for dinner. Crush was home! Home like Celie in the Color Purple. Crush ran to the top of the hill were she could see the big sky blue painted Victorian house in Madison County, Iowa.

Travis and Audrey Onyx, Crush's father and mother owned a great big dairy farm where they also bred cows to be sold as beef cattle for a source of income. The farm was passed down from generation to generation. It was recorded that Audrey's Great-Great Grand Parents were slaves, and their Masters loved them so, that they left all their property to them in their will to inherit because they could not conceive children of their own. As sad as it is, but yes, their slaves were the closet they ever had to family. Having hundreds of acres of land, and Dairy stock committees, the property value is now worth, in net, close to three hundred and fifty million dollars. Travis and Audrey Onyx were very wealthy black folk, especially for that time in the mid sixties.

Crush could see the covered old wooden bridge that lead to the road that would take her to the front porch. Under the porch was a stream too wide and too deep to cross by foot. Crush headed towards the bridge happy and free spirited anxiously wanting to see her parents again. Being in her dream state, Crush knew the difference between realty and what she was experiencing while being unable to move her body in the state of shock. Crush knew her parents died many years ago leaving her the millions to inherit. But it felt so good, that she ignored reality to relive that moment for just one more time. Crush ran faster and faster towards the bridge wanting this feeling never to end. As she ran, she laughed out loud as the grey fox squirrels scurried up the trees. Then out of nowhere, the biggest Eastern Cotton Tailed rabbit hopped in Crush's path.

Crush stopped in amazement, admiring the grey fluffy rabbit with cute white paws. She kneeled down to pick up the rabbit, when suddenly an ax came flying down at top speed cutting the rabbits head off. Blood splattered everywhere in all directions. Crush's face and white dress became drenched in rabbit blood. Crush looked up at the hands gripping the wooden handle only to see herself hovering over "her" shoulder wearing the same white dress and orange tank-top. The only thing missing was the blue and orange purple polka dot scarf around her neck.

"Bulls-eye! Did you see that shit Crush? Did you see that fucking shit? I took that mother fucker's head right off yo. I hope that wasn't Bugs Bunny yo. I liked that fucking rabbit, like for real though!"

Crush stood there trembling, blinking her eyes rapidly for a few seconds, then began to scream at the top of her lungs. "You killed him!! You-you....killed him! You BITCH! How did you get here? Where the hell did you come from ONYX?"

"I don't know myself Crush? There I was, in my lonely room doing my nails, reading a book, playing with my pussy, and BAM! I saw you acting like a fucking fool in the fields. So I followed you and decided to have some fun. I never saw you- I meant me-you know what I'm saying...US! You know, together at the same time? I haven't discussed the possibilities of this happening in those sessions with Dr. Big Dick Korvach. Ya know?"

Crush closed her eyes tightly and began to chant in a whispery voice.

"Onyx back to your lonely room!"
"Onyx back to your lonely room!"
"Onyx back to your lonely room!"

Opening her eyes after taking a deep breath, she was surprised to see Onyx gone and the bloody ax lying in the grass beside the decapitated rabbit's head.   Crush took another deep breath of relief. Then, (SMACKKK) Crush was hit so hard from a sucker punch, blood shot out of her mouth while spinning face first into the grass.

"HA-HA, you're such a fucking pussy Crush! I could get use to this shit here. Yes, this new physical touching shit? I don't know how, but fuck it. It's fun."

Crush wiped the blood from her mouth looking at Onyx standing there bobbing in a Boxer's motion waiting for the next bell to ring. But with a calm thought, and a soft whisper, crush mumbled..."NO", and (poof), Onyx disappeared into thin air and was gone. She placed both hands covering her face mumbling to herself again, "What the hell is going on?" removing her hands away, in a short breath, she realized she was no longer in the fields. She was in a room that was more familiar to her than any other room she's been in; Dr. Kenneth Korvach's office was the same as she'd remembered. Crush looked back and forth, side to side, for the face of a man who knew the answers to the mystery question now unveiled in her mind. She screamed as loud as she could in frenzy. "Dr. Korvach! Dr. Kenneth Korvach! Show yourself DAMNIT! YOU SON OF A BITCH! SHOW YOURSELF!"

With a blink of an eye that seemed to last a long time, Crush opened her eyes to see her best friend Tracy, and her long time lover Brian sitting beside her fast asleep in two hospital chairs. Sitting up in the bed, she lean over and pushed Tracy's head to see if she was, in fact, real and not a dream.

"WHAT THE FUCK!" Tracy said waking up in a bitch fit mood. Crush knew for sure she was no longer tumbling down the rabbit hole. Brian was awakened by the sound of Tracy's loud response from Crush pushing her head. Both of them rushed to her side with concern in their eyes.

"Crush, are you ok sweetie?" Brian asked as he brushed the back of his four fingers across Crush's face.

"Oh my God girl, you are like totally freaking me out right now. You're not smoking that crack shit, are you?" Tracy said in a joking manner. Brian looked at Tracy with his mouth wide open. Then he turned to Crush with one eyebrow up. "Well are you?" Crush rolled her eyes and put her middle finger up at the both of them.

Dr. Sanchez just so happened to be walking by when she heard the sound of laughter coming from Room 302. She walked inside with Crush's medical chart attached to a clip board. Tracy and Brian began to apologize to the doctor hoping they weren't doing anything wrong by having Crush laugh after coming out of a sudden state of shock. If in fact, that was what it was. Dr. Sanchez kindly asked Tracy and Brian to wait out in the waiting area while she took Crush's vitals. Doing so, Brian kissed Crush on the forehead and said in a whisper he'll be right outside. Tracy held her hand and said the same. As they exited the room, Sanchez took out her pocket flashlight and began to check Crush's pupils.

On their way to the waiting area, Brian asked Tracy if she wanted a hot cup of coffee from the vending machine down the hall. She answered with a "hell yea" as she sat her ass in those uncomfortable blue waiting seats. Brian continued to head down the hallway. As soon as Brian saw he was out of Tracy's view, he looked back with a serious look to make sure Tracy did not change her mind and decided to accompany him instead.

Making a quick left, he asked one of the hospital orderlies where he might be able to take a quick piss. The orderly pointed three doors down and on the right. He told Brian sarcastically, please make sure to wipe after himself. Brian looked at him weird and walked down the hall towards the restrooms.

Entering the restroom he found his way to the last available toilet stall. He pushed open the door with his foot not wanting to touch what appeared to be a slimy substance on the door. Unraveling as much toilet tissue as possible from its holder, he placed all the tissue around, and on top of the toilet seat in an attempt to not get the next mans urine on his clean pants. He pulled a black Sprint mobile phone from his pocket and began to dial. Sitting there tapping his foot on the floor waiting for the person he was calling to answer, he looked under the side stalls next to him to see if the area was clear for a private conversation. The person to his call picked up.

"Yes it's me sir! You-you told me to call if anything seemed strange in Crush's behavior and this is pretty strange sir!" As Brian's voice echoed through the empty bathroom stalls all his short and simple conversation consisted of, "Yes sir! No sir! I'll do whatever I have to do sir! I'm not sure sir? I'm on it sir!" Just as he ended his call, he noticed a moving shadow under the stall door making him suspect someone was listening in on his conversation. No one could see the 9 millimeter pistol strapped in its ankle-velcro gun holder attached to Brian's right leg. He slowly lifted the pant leg pulling the pistol out and stood up pointing the gun towards the ceiling as he slowly opened the stall door.

Meanwhile back in Room 302, Dr. Sanchez removes the IV from Crush's left hand and places a band-aid over the sore and bruised area. "So Dr. Sanchez, what is the problem? Is there some reason to why my body would just shut down like that?"

Crush pretended not to know the answer to her own question. Not wanting to mention what had taken place a few hours ago, she knew she would sound more than crazy, but as crazy does. Dr. Sanchez put her Gucci specs on and pulled the chair closer to the side of Crush's bed. Crush was sitting up in her hospital gurney with both legs hanging off the bed facing Dr. Sanchez waiting to hear what seemed of great importance.

"Ms. Onyx, I had to search for medical records or medical history about you on my computer. I had some problems at first. It said medically classified? I took some short cuts. But what I found was that your last family Doctor was Dr. Kenneth Korvach? At first I didn't realize your last name, but I do remember many classes I had to attend on his work during my med school period. His work was amazing! Then a few years back, before his mysterious death and disappearance, he was treating a patient with a dual-split personality disorder. The patient was an F.B.I. suspect for several murders but she was never convicted because of the psychoanalysis therapy reports submitted to the F.B.I. by Dr. Korvach. She was placed in his care and was never heard from again. Five years ago—that was you!! Now is there something you want to talk about? I can swear by medical oath as your doctor, whatever you say to me from this moment is on a strict and confidential basis. Ms. Crush Onyx, I'm a Big fan of your studies you see…………

CHAPTER THREE:

"ONLY THE DEAD ARE INSTITUTIONALIZED"

The fourth floor at F.B.I. headquarters in Langley Virginia was loud with phones ringing, and Federal Bureau Agents Candice Sums, and Michelle Blake, frustrated with large stacks of case files placed on their desks. As they sit opposite to each other in their small cubicles, the two woman who find themselves throwing rocks at the "Glass Ceiling" in the F.B.I. work force, continue to make their way up the Bureau's ladder, solving as many caseloads as possible, hoping one day to become a beacon for other woman to follow in the field of Law Enforcement.

Candice Sums was a good old fashion country white girl. Blonde hair, Bahama Blue water colored eyes, about 120 pounds, five foot seven inches, beautiful and intelligent. Candice graduated top of her class for F.B.I.'s Profile and Criminal Behavioral studies of the most dangerous

Serial Killers known to man. Candice was the investigating agent seven years ago for the Ms. Crush Onyx murders. Along with her childhood friend and 12 year partner, Michelle Blake. They were sent to Iowa State to study patterns that lead to the brutal and horrifying murders of more than fifty bodies found state wide. All clues tracing back to Crush Onyx. Knowing about her mental birth disorder, Candice Sums became obsessed chasing Crush, body after body. Still with no proof to present in the court of Law, trying to have Crush convicted for her onslaught of murderous escapades, she was taken off the case. She then had an order of protection placed on her by Dr. Kenneth Korvach to stay clear away from Crush.

Even five years later, Agents Candice and Michelle clearly remembers the day "Onyx" presented herself in physical form through Crush's body when being interrogated and questioned about her being connected to those horrible murders. Both Agents were horrified to know that such a creature could exist inside the mind and body of Crush. They questioned how she could still be allowed to walk and live free amongst innocent civilians.

Michelle Blake; was a very attractive black woman about 130 pounds, light brown skinned, dark brown eyes with a short hair cut, 5'5". Michelle's more aggressive attitude compliments her partnership with Candice. Michelle's father was also an F.B.I. agent who was killed in the field during a major undercover drug sting in Washington D.C., during her earlier teenage years. As a child Michelle was defiant to the day of his death. Giving her father the shit–fit every chance she could for never being home while her and her mother attended school plays, dance class, piano lessons, and even missing her graduations. Shortly after her father's death and full of guilt, Michelle and Candice both country girls born and raised in Charlottesville, Virginia, made a pack that they would join the best law enforcement team and together, they will put dangerous criminals behind bars were they belonged. They haven't separated since that pack was made.

Candice and Michelle were going over their notes and files, hot on the trail of a new and unique serial killer the bureau named the "Black Butterfly" birth name Tabitha Black. "Michelle! There's got to be reason why Black Butterfly keeps leaving these easy clues and evidence for us to catch her?" Candice said as she gazed at the pile of photos on the desk. One photo of a man totally naked hanging from a rope upside down tied to his chandelier. His arms were skinned from his shoulders to his wrists. The eyes from his head were surgically removed from their sockets and placed in his nut–sacks...replacing his genitals. The skin from his arms was replaced with colorful butterfly wings, giving the image of a tattooist art work of a jigsaw puzzle. Black Butterfly's trade mark was leaving her victim's limbs covered in colorfully coded designs to solve. Any body parts that were skinned from her victims were replaced by a sleeve of real butterfly wings.

"Listen Candice, why don't we fly over to Canada with the proper warrants and arrest this sick bitch? We know where she's at! What the fuck is the problem?"

"Michelle, let's not forget about you-know-who! I don't want to make the same mistake twice. We almost lost our jobs behind chasing that chick." Candice said as she flung the photos on top of the desk with an attitude.

"Candice, it's been five damn years already. Let Crush Onyx go already! You are right about one thing, us 'almost' losing 'our' jobs. The woman has mental issues, so what! Plus you had us all chasing a ghost phantom. And I know it's hard to accept but------

Candice cut Michelle off by standing up and pointing in her face. "BUT FUCKING WHAT MICHELLE? You still think I was bugging the fuck out? What are you saying Michelle! I'm fucking incompetent? You're supposed to be my best friend before my partner! You got nerve to insinuate----"

It was Michelle's turn to cut Candice off. Placing her elbows on the desk and then rolling her eyes up in her head and sucking her teeth. "Let's not do this Candice. Why don't you take a chill pill! Or go get some coffee, a salad, something to calm your attitude down. I'm not the enemy here, and I'm not insinuating anything here."

"Yes Agent Sums! Why don't you go and calm yourself down! Displaying that kind of attitude won't go well in this office!" another voice shouted over the cubical, the voice of the Unit's Supervisor.

Candice gave Michelle a look of sorrow for the way she snapped at her but Crush Onyx made a home underneath her skin like a parasite. "Onyx" haunted her dreams for five long years, questioning herself for her mistakes. Where did I go wrong? What did I miss? How did I screw up the case? And the death of Dr. Korvach, and whether Onyx would ever resurface?

She lifted her head coming out of a few seconds of thought, smiled at the Unit Supervisor giving him a hand-to-the-head salute. Grabbing a set of keys from her purse she unlocked her bottom desk draw and pulled out an old and personal file on Dr. Korvach and Crush Onyx. The label pasted on the manila folder read "closed case reports". She grabbed her black silk Donna Karen blazer off the back of her seat alone with her favorite brown suede cowgirl hat.

"Are you coming Michelle?

"Sure Candice. Let me grab these photos and then we can compare the notes we got on home girl B.B."

Before Candice or Michelle could get their papers together, the Unit Supervisor David Allgood shouted across the room from his office door made of sound proof glass.

"Sums! Blake! The chief dropped the green light on your warrants to pick up Black Butterfly. Suit-up and take a small team with you. The chopper is fueled and ready for takeoff. You ladies know the drill. This is that break you've both been waiting for. CHOP-CHOP!" Candice and Michelle ran back to their desk quickly putting the files back in the draws.

Checking their weapons on the way up in the elevator they were met at the roof of the F.B.I. headquarters. Waiting there was a team of five men, heavily armed and passing them bullet-proof vests of their own to wear for protection. The sound of the helicopters blade ripping the wind filled their ears as they climbed inside and strapped themselves in for the journey to Canada to apprehend Black Butterfly. They began to brief their team on how to approach the capture of such a violent killer. They advised them to use skill and caution. Two Agents lost their lives trying to invade the last residence of Tabitha Black. One Agent was a female. She was spared. Only found with her head decapitated. The other was male. Black Butterfly went to work on him. By the time they put all the body parts together to identify him; it took nearly two months before his family could give him a decent funeral.

A few hours later, Candice, the unit team, and Michelle circled the residence where Black Butterfly was told by several leads that she would be at this address. Candice and Michelle crept up the front porch with weapons drawn, and signaled the team to smash the front door open. Making their entrance rushing in with caution, M16s with inferred beams and scopes searched for any body movement on site. As the team whispered "Clear!" around every turn, and smoothly maneuvering from room to room on the bottom level, Candice and Michelle were making their way up the flight of steps to the top level of the house.

The house was neatly furnished with plush leather couches and beautiful oak wood cabinets. The oak wood floors were shined and buffed, pictures of what appeared to be a happy family covered the walls leading up to the top level. Michelle stopped in mid-step when her eyes locked and could not turn away from one picture that stood out of place to her. Sure there were pictures of Tabitha and her family, mother, sister, brother and father of course. There were pictures of a few kids' faces, perhaps nephews, nieces, cousins.

Michelle signaled the team behind her with an opened hand gesture displaying STOP! She then grabbed Candice stopping her from going any further because she was lead. Candice with her weapon pointed up and focused on her next step, looked at Michelle like she was crazy for stopping her. The Unit team also looked puzzled through their black face masks with tinted black goggles and body gear giving the same look. Michelle pointed at the picture on the wall that caused the team to stop in their pursuit.

Candice could not stop her face from turning beet red. Her eyes widened open. Her mouth opened wider with breath escaping as if she saw a ghost. They both lost all their logical sensory when focused on the picture of Crush and Tabitha hugging each other with smiles on their faces and on the very same porch in which they made their entry. The picture was very old in date. The picture had to be taken while Crush and Tabitha were in their twenties. Candice noticed the butterfly print sundress that Crush was wearing in the picture. They both were smiling as if they were best of friends. Stuck in the moment, two shots were fired from a silencer into the back of Agent Candice, spinning her around and sending her tumbling down the steps crashing into Michelle; causing both agents to lose balance and fall half a flight.

Shots rang out from M16 machine guns in a matter of seconds up in the direction of the top banister. Wood chips flew everywhere. The team leader screamed GO-GO-GO! As two unit men ran to the top of the stairs. Looking in both directions almost reaching the last step, the two unit men met their fate. Infer-red beams placed at the base of the step triggered a small C4 bomb at their ankles, strong enough just killing them both on impact. Smoke and flying pieces of the staircase covered the three remaining unit men holding Agents Candice and Michelle as they carried the ladies to safety making their way back to the front door to exit. Candice being dragged by her upper chest still groggy from the shots she took to the back, her eyes focused on the picture of Crush and Tabitha in the frame now cracked from the explosion and lying beside her dragging legs. She reached for the frame with her soot-covered hands, and took it with her as the unit men continued to scream, "MOVE IT-MOVE IT!!" While falling off the porch and onto the lawn.

Michelle's face was also covered with soot, coughing and screaming back at the three unit men. "DON'T LET HER GO OUT THE BACK DOOR!" as she checked to see if her partner was alright. Kneeling down to aid Candice, Michelle checked the two bullet holes in the blazer. The bullet-proof vest did its job. Candice was not bleeding. She was hurt, but not injured.

"How much was this Donna Karen blazer?"

"Fuck you Michelle!"

Candice pulled the hidden picture from her waist line and threw it at Michelle hitting her in the chest.

"Now please explain to me why the hell Crush Onyx is all buddy-buddy with psycho sis Tabitha Black?"

"Well I'll be damn!" was the only thing Michelle could say.

Candice had her head planted in Michelle's lap. On reflex, Michelle lifted her weapon up and spun around to see Black Butterfly about five feet away standing there behind them. There she was, six feet tall, looking as beautiful as Ms. Kimora Lee Simmons the model. Just so happening to be wearing a matching Baby Phat yellow spaghetti string halter camisole, with a yellow cut-out skirt, her legs were smooth and muscular defined, with a pair of black wedges by the shoe designer Giuseppe Zanotti. Her feet were planted evenly spread on the grass lawn.

"PUT YOUR FUCKING HANDS UP TABITHA OR I WILL SHOOT YOUR SICK ASS DEAD WHERE YOU STAND!!" Michelle screamed as she pointed her weapon dead center at her head.

"Do you think that by me dying today, it will stop the work of Dr. Kenneth Korvach?" Black Butterfly said with a calm and smooth seductive voice. Looking right pass Michelle and focusing on Candice. Candice reached for her weapon, but realized it was not in her holster.

"I SAID GET DOWN NOW!! NOW!! NOW DAMN IT!!" Agent Michelle continued to scream at the top of her lungs.

"Onyx was too smart for Dr. Korvach. She knew he would try to separate her from Crush. So she took us under her wings with love. She showed us all how to be free. Free from your laws of wealth. Free from your laws of sexual gender! Free from your laws that binds humanity from making our own choices and decisions on how we should live. Your society has put restraints on life since the beginning of time. Your so called laws of a God who never shows himself in flesh. Spirit? What spirit does one have, when we're told what to eat, what to wear, whom we shall have sexual relations with! A God who allows war, racism, disease, death! We the followers of the Sand Box will give new meaning to those laws! We decide who shall fall under for their misdeeds! I am just one who is willing to die for that cause Agent Blake and Agent Sums!"

The remaining three unit men came from both directions left and right of the house pointing their M16 machine guns at Black Butterfly.

"Let my death, bring life to my teacher and mentor!" she whispered and began to walk towards Michelle and Candice with a smile from ear to ear. She in-fact welcomed death with open arms. Without hesitation shots rang out from automatic weapons filling Tabitha's body with more than 113 bullets clear to the chest, and 5 to the face. She shook as her bones and flesh was ripped to shreds. When her body hit the grass lawn, Michelle, Candice, and the three unit men faces were filled with a touch of sorrow. Their jobs are based on instincts and most definitely filled with danger. But they are not executioners. Her bloody and lifeless body lying on the lawn, eyes wide open, looking up at the clouds, Tabitha was consulted by her only friend, an orange and black winged butterfly spiraled down in a circular motion landing on her forehead for only a few seconds before taking flight. Born free! Born beautiful! Born to fly! Born to die! Agent Michelle turned her head in the direction of the unit men throwing both arms in the air in disgust.

"Do any of you fucking assholes know what protocol means? Apprehend suspect! Alive if possible! Then we question! She was fucking unarmed, and non-threatening your fucking pricks!"

Sirens flared and rang out as the local authorities came swerving around every corner in their patrol cars. Fire trucks made their way through the now swarming crowd of neighbors as they watched in amazement while Tabitha's house went up in flames. By the time the fire was under control, the lawn was filled with news vans from almost every channel known to cable, CNN, ABC, NBC, UPN, WB, and all Canadian channels as well. Candice and Michelle sat inside the local ambulance guarded by unit men. They could see the pushing cameras that belonged to reporters trying to get their exclusive shot and statements on the capture of Black Butterfly.

As lights continued to flash from hand held cameras at Michelle and Candice, they both began to shake their heads back and forth knowing what was going to happen next. Two seconds more without a breath lost, the back door flung open with a thrust to see Unit Supervisor David Allgood pissed off. He climbed into the ambulance taking a seat opposite of both agents. The three unit men outside guarding the ambulance from reporters gave each other a quick eye to eye contact and continued to block the door as instructed.

"Did you two nitwits observe the families who live across the street watch you shoot and kill an unarmed woman down on her lawn? DID YOU! I think I specifically said, APPREHEND!! NOT KILL!!" and let's not forget about the ethnic background!"

Looking at Agent Michelle, Allgood continues, "THAT'S RIGHT AGENT BLAKE! A FUCKING BLACK WOMAN GUNNED DOWN ON HER FUCKING LAWN!! You don't think the bureau has enough press rumors about racial profiling? DO YOU!" Turning his head in Candice direction, "AND YOU, I'm ready to turn your fucking papers in for your own psych evaluation. Are you still getting personal on this shit?"

Candice reached into the inside pocket of her blazer to retrieve the picture of Crush Onyx and Tabitha Black. "Sir, I think you should take a look at something we found." Allgood cut Candice off...

"The only damn thing I need to see is your reports on my desk tonight! TONIGHT! Not tomorrow. Is that clear! IS THAT CLEAR AGENTS BLAKE AND SUMS!?"

"YES SIR!" was the only thing you heard from both agents.

Allgood kicked the double doors to the ambulance open with his foot and walk over to the press cameras to give a statement. Candice and Michelle stared at each other with a silent glare. They both made their

exit from the ambulance and made their way back to the chopper waiting to take them back to Langley headquarters.

In mid flight Michelle leans over towards Candice and whispers in her ear. "Do you believe the nerve of that prick? I say we file our reports, and then put in for personal time and find our little friend Crush Onyx". Candice gave Michelle a high five and replied. "Now that's what the fuck I'm talking about!"

CHAPTER FOUR:

"CALM BEFORE THE STORM"

1:45 am. The hospital is still flooded with people and the sound of speakers blaring, "Paging Dr.-stat!" Paging Nurse stat!" as orderlies scurry patients around on beds, the TV show "Grey's Anatomy" can give you a vision of what it's like at New York City hospitals during the summer months.

Brian Century slowly opened the bathroom stall door. His eyes ready to catch any sudden movement from the unknown listener. He could see two mirrors on the bathroom wall across from the stall he was in. Brian squinted his eyes to focus, hoping the mirrors would cast a reflection and give away the unwanted parties view. The mirrors were too stained and glossy to see through clearly, probably the result of poor housekeeping and years of non-maintenance work.

Before Brian could make a fast break exit out of the bathroom stall, two well dressed black men entered the restroom. Pushing the door with their loud conversation, Brian quickly closed the stall door and put his 9 mm pistol back in its ankle holster. Brian could hear one of the men make a comment about the young Nurses Aid's beautiful round shaped ass as the other agreed. He flushed the toilet giving the impression that he had just finished unloading. As he closed the stall door behind him, he made his way to the glossy mirrors to wash his hands before getting back to Tracy and Crush, who was probably wondering about his whereabouts.

Looking down the crowded hospital hallway, Brian scanned each passing face hoping to recognize anyone that might have been giving him a suspicious glare. With no luck, he continued down the hall and approached Tracy. She was still sitting and reading a XXL magazine with her legs crossed.

"Wow Brian. I guess the food on the plane doesn't sit too well with your stomach huh." Tracy said as she read on without looking up.

Brian moved the oversized Leather Gabbana bag off the seat beside Tracy and plopped himself in the seat. Tracy began to notice the distracted look on Brian's face as he looked in both directions numerous times.

"Umm, Brian, are you ok?"

"Excuse me?" Brian's face jotted back quickly back in Tracy's direction.

"No! I mean, yes. Just wondering what's going on with Dr. Sanchez and Crush. Has she come back with info on Crush since you've been sitting here?"

"No, not yet" Tracy turned to the next page.

Still in Room 302, Crush sat on the edge of her bed with a smirk on her face. After Sanchez told her about her dark past that she had hoped would not follow her, it was no more of a surprise to her compared to what had happened down in the garage before going into shock? Crush took the tip of her tongue and ran it across her gum line while giving Sanchez a serious look into her eyes.

"Excuse me Dr. Sanchez! But, how dare you come in here and bring up my past history and judge me. My boyfriend is a well respected Lawyer from Iowa State! Maybe he should be in here before I answer anymore questions!"

Crush folded her arms placing them over her breast. Dr. Sanchez calmly took her Gucci frames off and placed them into the pocket of her coat.

"Ms. Onyx! I can assure you that I did not mean to offend you, nor, disrespect you in any way!" Dr. Sanchez put a concerned look on her face as she reached over and gently placed her hand on Crush's shoulder.

"May I call you Crush? My first name is Karen. I just want to talk woman to woman. Let me tell you a little bit about myself. I have scholarly degrees in all fields Crush. I have my B.S, M.D, and my Ph.D. I used to be a big fan of Kenneth Korvach's research work, until, sorry to say, all the news press he was getting about you being his patient. Something does not sit right in my gut about that situation with you and him. I'm not supposed to say this, but I believe he was the cause of you being so misguided?"

Crush rose up slowly, and walked herself over to the room window. Pushing the curtains back, she began to gaze out onto the City streets, quietly mumbling to herself. The window rattled from the base projected by Luxury cars bumping there Hip-Hop tunes coming from high definition speakers. With her left hand holding the curtain open, she began to use her right hand to rub her temple then turning back to Dr. Sanchez.

"How do I know I can trust you Karen? How can I trust anyone, when I can't even trust myself? I had an interesting life. The only thing I want to do is take a hot bath, and gather my thoughts. So if it's ok with you, I would like to continue this another day and go home now!"

Dr. Sanchez took a deep breath and walked over to Crush as she turned back around and continued to look out the window. She reached inside her doctor's lab coat and pulled out a card with her number and info on it. She told Crush that she would be available to talk anytime, and Crush could call her at home if needed. Crush was then caught off guard when Karen gave her a hug, told her she was being discharged, could go home and to get plenty of rest. After Karen had left the room, Crush sat and waited as Tracy entered the room carrying her bag stuffed with cloths and a pair of sneakers for her to go home in.

"Oh my God Tracy, what did you do to my dolce bag?"

"Listen, Miss Alice in Wonderland. I'm tired! I've been sitting down so long, my ass feels like it's been Fucked by a 12 inch dildo. I think I'm getting my period, and your boyfriend acts like he has a cocaine addiction, and now you want to complain? BITCH PLEASE!"

Crush chuckled as she snatched the bag from Tracy. She then pulled her cloths out of the bag; a grey tight Sean John velour sweat-suit, a white spaghetti string halter top, and a pair of gray on white puma sneakers. After Crush was fully dressed and tied her sneaker strings, she asked if Brian was okay. Tracy smiled and said he was fine and he had gone back to her place to run her a bath and cook her some real food. While on their way out, Tracy continued to give Crush an ear full on how men are so damn impatient and how Brian should have waited.

Finally reaching outside the hospital walls, the cool summer breeze and the noise was music to Crush's ears. Tracy's Mercedes Benz was parked across the street from the hospital. She gave Crush a ride home and gave her a big hug when she pulled up to the building.

Crush was sluggish and tired as she got off the elevator carrying her Dolce bag in one hand and her keys in the other. She had given Brian an extra set to her condo being he was the one who found it for her to purchase at the reasonable price that was given. Entering her apartment closing the door behind her, the hallway leading through the living room to her bedroom was dimmed down to a soothing mood. Crush made her way down the two steps that lead into her sunken-in living room area and placed her bag on the plush couch. She quickly scanned the area when she heard the soft music of Gerald Levert being played from her room located at the far right end of the hallway.

Crush put a huge smile on her face and walked down the hallway to her room. The room door was half opened and she could see the silhouette shadows projected from the burning candles as the music got louder and louder as she approached. Crush pushed the door open slowly and bit her bottom lip softly and seductively when she saw Brian standing there bare chest. All she could think about was rubbing him all over. She noticed he was wearing a black pair of unisex draw sting silk charmeuse lounge pants, and holding a glass of cognac in his hand. He was reading the back of the CD case before realizing Crush was standing there staring.

The silence was thick between them both while the candle light danced their shadows on the wall. They stared for a few more seconds at each other with lust and anticipated passion. Crush shifted her eyes in the direction of her dresser and noticed all the wonderful little items. She smiled even harder when she saw her favorite irresistible and delicious silky oils that impart a very delicate scent and tingly warmth when applied to the body. Caress a few drops on whatever spot one desires, then blow gently to release their powers; and WHOA! Then her eyes shifted to the right of the bed. There she gazed upon this enticing sheer peek-a-boo baby doll with adjustable satin straps featuring sheer nylon with ruffle trim, satin tie open bra cups, and matching G-string teddy set. Crushes idea of a hot bath and relaxing completely flew right out the fucking window. Between her legs became moist, and her heart began to pick up speed. Crush was ready for hard passion! And that was that!

Brian took a sip from his glass and walked smoothly and cool over to Crush placing his left hand on her right breast and began to caress her nipple in a circular rotation making them perk from its warmth. Crush could smell Brian's breathe as he whispered in her ear softly. "I'm going to poor you a drink. And when I get back, I'm sure you'll have that sexy shit on so we can relax." Crush closed her eyes and could feel his erected cock pressed against her thigh through her sweat suit. Brian walked away leaving her wanting it even more. She ran over towards her bed tearing her clothes off frantically in a comical way. Re-entering the bedroom with two glasses half full with cognac, Brian walked over to

Crush. As requested, Crush was wearing the complete teddy set brushing her hair sitting with her back towards him. Crush let out a soft moan when Brian's hand shifted under her arm and began to squeeze her soft breast through the bra. Crush had a beautifully shaped ass like the video vixen Melissa Ford aka, Asteria Rabbit. She began to grind its fluffiness on his rock hard dick.

Brian rubbed along the side of her small waistline making his way down to her pubic hairs. Kissing Crush on her shoulder gave her a chill that sent a shiver up her spine and shock waves to the center of her thighs. With both his arms around her waist he planted his fingers on her clitoris, pushing two of them in her pussy, Crush spread her thighs further apart for better penetration. Crush was now super wet and ready for love making she whispered out "I love you" then Brian pulled the G-string to the side, lifted her up, positioned her and slowly entered her from behind. For twenty minutes Brian had Crush's ass bouncing up and down as he continued to thrust his hard cock in and out her dripping wet pussy. With his silk pants dropped to his ankles, he pulled out of her and spun her around pulling her close chest to chest. Crush had her eyes closed in ecstasy dripping in sweat, her teddy glued to her body. Without opening her eyes and her hands planted on Brian's sweaty chest, taking short breaths, she kneeled down on both knees grabbing his still erected cock, and with her juices still wet and warm, she began to suck on the soft tip.

Brian continued to moan out loud as he held her head and bobbed it front to back as she deep throated his cock. After 10 minutes of some serious head, he whispered "Let's get on the bed". She chuckled as she pushed him off balance and onto the oversized bed. Gerald Levert's CD was now over leading into an Old school slow Jam mixed CD by DJ Kid Kapri; Rick James & Tina Marie "Fire & Desire" duet came blazing out the surround sound speakers. "That's my shit!" Crush said while she climbed on top of Brian ready to ride him Cowgirl style. "OH MY DAMN! This pussy is insane from every angle I hit it in!" Brian said while he leveled his dick in the direction of Crush's wet enter spot. They both laughed for a second as Crush slid him into her. She rode Brian for thirty minutes before he exploded his cream load up inside her. She screamed out louder in deep climax. "I'm CUMMIN! OH MY GOD!" they both shivered and clinched each other tight. Crush sat there on his cock for a few more seconds still shivering in short waves one after another. Lying down beside him, they took a few more minutes to just cuddle. Dripping with sweaty bodies, they made their way to the shower.

Standing in the bathroom with their naked bodies, Brain complimented the beauty in the designing and feature in the room. Two sinks, one large glass walk in shower, Full size bath tub, glass cabinets the size of a five foot person. Crush had large fluffy beach towels on four chrome holders, with matching hand wash cloths; the floors were large Black and White checkered tiles. Although, she still had imported floor carpets from China under each sink, the bathroom still had space for a plush white sitting lounge couch to relax in on each side of the shower were 10 foot chrome bathrobe poles with hooks to hang. After taking their shower, she rubbed his back dry and told him to get some rest so she can dry her hair. He gave her a kiss and made his way to the bedroom. 4:00 a.m., 15 minutes had gone by. She sat there in the mirror with the door closed, and the sound of the blow dryer pumping its heat to straighten her kinks out. She started to think about the past day. Looking in the mirror at her reflection, the images of the two teenage girls Leto and Asteria's faces were imprinted in her memory. She tried to convince herself it was just a prank, and some one's sick try of making jokes of her past life. But she couldn't! They looked just like her in every way, every feature. As much as Crush wanted to believe herself, she knew the only person who would have answers to those questions, honestly, and open with no regards to her feelings would be... ONYX!

She got up from the soft plush white sofa couch, locked the door, and also knew Brian was a very hard sleeper and would not hear her talking to herself in the bathroom alone. Sitting back on the sofa couch, she took a deep breath, closed her eyes and concentrated on opening up the lonely room located in the far corner of her cerebrum. In seconds, her mind opened up.

"Well, well, well! I can still taste Brian's cum oozing down your throat. Why didn't you take it up the ass Crush? I loved getting our ass pounded out. That big fucking dick just in and out our ass! Mmmm, so gooood! I use to take three dicks at a time Crush. But you're not me, but you are me, oops." Onyx let out a laugh that made Crush cringe.

CHAPTER FIVE:

"*ONYX 101- WALK WITH ME*"

THEORY OF PSYCHOANALYSIS; Psychoanalytic theory has, and, **fundamentally change the traditional conceptions of the manner in which the Human mind functions, of the role played in human life by instinctual drives, and of the nature of illness. The Unconscious; the first of Sigmund Freud's innovations was his recognition of unconscious psychic processes that follow laws different from those that govern conscious experience. Under the influence of the Unconscious, thoughts and feelings that belong together may be shifted or displaced out of context; two disparate condensed into one.**

After Crush had let Onyx out of her lonely room, and hearing her make that stupid comment, she opened her eyes and sucked her teeth in disgust. She could hear Onyx, but could not see her in shape, or physical form. Onyx was just a born mental malfunction in her id, ego, or super ego. Crush walked herself over to the bathroom mirror and continued to blow dry her hair. She wouldn't let Onyx see her panic. Onyx was very sneaky, and able to find ways to retrieve information to use against Crush in order to start useless conversations, just to avoid being locked in the lonely room.

Normally Crush would entertain in conversation with Onyx, but only under extreme boredom. The situation was becoming more complex. Onyx was finding ways to manipulate the laws of being bound to her room. First; she somehow interacted with her in a dream state. How? Now she's actually physically feeling sexual sensations through her Body, and visually seeing who, and how it was being done. Crush had to be smarter in her approach into finding out.

"What's up Onyx?" She said in a casual tone. "I like anal sex. I guess Brian wasn't in the mood. It seems you enjoyed it. I'm not sure on how you felt that? But care to explain that shit? Crush let out a soft chuckle to pretend she was ok with it, and not to sound confused or upset.

"I don't know! I told you before. There I was, in the dark, and-oh baby! I just started shivering all over-my-body."

"Yea I know what you mean Onyx. Brian does have that magic stick."

Crush put the blow dryer down and rolled her eyes at her reflection in the mirror. She was sick to her stomach at the fact that she had to continue this corny roll-play with Onyx.

"Anywayzzzz Crush! I know you're not here to talk to me, so why don't you just spit it out with your punk ass! You want to know what the dilly-o is with all the new shit happening between me and you. Am I correct, shit face?"

Crush gritted her teeth together and answered in a growling tone. "Yes Onyx. You are so smart!" in a sarcastic tone she answered.

"Don't fucking get cutesy with me, you fucking bitch! I'm trying to be fucking nice, and you want to ruin shit by acting like a sarcastic cunt. I don't know how bitch! It just happens!" Crush took a deep breath and began to pace back and forth. The silence was thick for a few seconds.

"I'm sorry Crushie Pooh. I get besides ourselves sometimes. But I do have one idea? Want to know what it is sweetie?"

Crush stopped pacing back and forth placing her hands on her hips. Crush became suspicious when she had realized that Onyx would never apologize behind anything she said to her. She was definitely up to something! What?

"Idea huh, what idea is that Onyx?" she took a seat on her sofa chair and sat back to hear what Onyx had to say.

"I was thinking we could try that physical appearance thing again? You know, when you pulled me into your dream? I believe you were living a moment from our past. If that's correct, then maybe we can show each other some things about our separate selves from the past? Kind of like getting to know one another a little bit better."

Crush stood up and walked to the mirror. She then whispered at her reflection. "Are you fucking crazy, so you could beat the shit out of me, NO FUCKING WAY?"

"Ok then. I promise, Psycho's honor, I won't fuck with you on this one. I just want to show you a few things that might give you a perspective as to why I am the way that I am. I'm sure you would love to see what the good Dr. Kenneth Korvach was doing to us. And I can show you a few other things too." Sounding devilish.

"I don't know about that Onyx. You always have some angle!"
"Pussy"
"Onyx, listen to me.."
"Pussy-pussy-pussy" Onyx repeated.

"OKAY! Fine, the minute you start some shit, I swear I will lock you in that fucking room. The next time you get out, we will be 80 years old, crippled, and getting our ass wiped by abusive orderlies."

"Deal, but you have to vision us together in a neutral zone. I'm guessing you have to create a new room? Something like, a common center."

"I get the image Onyx. Just a minute, and be quiet."

Crush splashed some water on her face from the sink and took a seat on the sofa couch to concentrate. Her hands began to shake from being nervous. She also knew it would be dangerous to try something like that without proper and professional guidance. She had to start somewhere. Darkness was all around the image in her mind. Although her eyes were closed from the outside, her eyes were opened inside her mind. She found herself standing surrounded in space, no color, no objects, just all white. No walls, no doors, nothing to see but endless bright white space. Looking like the waiting area to get into heaven. She turned around in a complete circle looking for Onyx. She heard Onyx calling out to her. She could not see her, but the voice sounded faded with a slight far distant echo. Then she heard it again. This time a bit closer, *"Crush concentrate you stupid bitch!"* Crush chuckled at the fact that, Onyx will always be Onyx. No matter where or what the circumstances may be. She closed her eyes harder to concentrate and focus more on the task, but what she felt was a sudden energy pull from her soul. Opening her eyes, feeling a little dizzy, there was Onyx!

They were staring at each other in silence. Looking at themselves from head to toe, dressed in the same out-fits like identical twins. They were wearing some serious expensive shit. Their taste in fashion did not differ. Even in two separate mental identities. They both were wearing Chocolate brown Bianca sweaters, stretch cashmere T-necks by "Brunello Cicinelli", Italy: $598. A Chocolate brown, Johnston's cashmere, hand nit, 3/14 chalet sweater, Scotland: $1,498. A pair of Blue "Roxie jeans: $296, and a pair of Chocolate leather and stretch suede over the knee boots Italy: $1,598.

"SHIT, I look good. Damn I'm a fine bitch!" Onyx said grabbing her crotch like she was a Hip-Hop B-Boy.

Crush stood there looking around from left to right, up and down in a circular motion.

"Yea, I guess it's a sub-conscious image of how I would dress myself? Now what do we do from here Onyx."

Not paying attention to Onyx, she was side kicked in her back, causing her to drop to her knees in pain. Onyx grabbed Crush by her ponytail from the back. Leaned her head forward, leaving her throat exposed. Crush felt the cold blade of a machete across her throat. Crush on her knees, and Onyx staring down, Crush said in a low tone swallowing spit.

"What are you going to do now Onyx, kill me? The body can't live without the mind stupid ass!"

"Yes, yes, yes indeed. You are right about that Crush. The body cannot live without your mind! SHIT!"

Letting go of Crush, Onyx dropped the machete and took two steps back away from Crush. After Crush stood up from being on her knees, she kicked Onyx between the legs in her private part. Onyx dropped to her knees as well.

"I'm really getting fucking tired of your bullshit BITCH! Keep snuffing me from behind like the coward you are, and we will be two fighting bitches up in here Mother Fucker! I am not a fucking punk Onyx!"

"That's all you got Crush? That's it?" Onyx stood up and began to laugh real hard at Crush, as if she wasn't hurt at all. *"Ok Crush. Now let's see if my idea works. I'm going to concentrate and take you somewhere I've been. You want to see when I fucked your Ex boyfriend in high school? Ha, I'm just playing. Hold on to your tits, let's go!"* Onyx closed her eyes tightly, while Crush watched closely to see what was about to happen.

The white room began to swirl the form of a black hole. Colors began to blend around Crush and Onyx in the middle. Voices echoed in and out like whispers. Some voices were recognizable to Crush, and some were not. Crush began to see images and flashes of her parents in various settings yelling at her, and then some of her being hugged. Probably being disciplined for something Onyx had done before her parents realized she had a mental illness or should we say "ONYX", Crush's split personality.

She was in amazement as she watched. She knew those images were not only memories of her own, but memories of Onyx reliving past events in the same body. It was like a thousand televisions, with no frames, just scenes over lapping one after another. She covered her mouth with both hands, when she focused on one scene of Dr. Korvach receiving a blow-job from Onyx in his office behind his work desk. She couldn't believe what she was seeing. Her face, her body, and the man her parents trusted to protect her., teach her and help her get that evil personality out of her head. She was more saddened, than upset. Dr. Kenneth Korvach has been her therapist since she could remember from the age of four. Although he never touched Crush in that way sexually, he would seem more protective about Crush when it came to boys. Crush turned to Onyx with tears in her eyes wanting to question, when Onyx put her hand gently on her mouth stopping her from speaking. For a moment, Crush thought she saw sorrow in Onyx's eyes.

"It just breaks your poor little heart Crush doesn't it; well I'm not as sympathetic to your pain. You were treated like a fucking princess, while the good Doctor fucked me every session we had! He told me that I

was more special to him than you. His lies, filthy fucking lies. Just like mom and dad. But I showed them how special I really was! And now I will show you too!"

As Crush blinked her eyes, the scene changed to a full set. She found herself standing in what appeared to be a High School class room she was not familiar with. Surrounded by a room full of students sitting at their desks talking among themselves playing girly games, laughing at each other's jokes, and dressed in Red and Black checkered miniskirts with white cotton collard button-up shirts, with small bow-ties to match. Catholic all girl's school, Crush presumed. She could not remember ever being a student at this private school. Then she saw herself sitting in the far corner at a desk. But it wasn't her, it was Onyx! Two Indian pony-tail braids, one leg crossed over the other, knee high white stockings, and a pair of brown Penny Loafer shoes.

Onyx appeared totally oblivious to Crush's presences in the class room. Onyx was oblivious to the rest of the class as well. The ringing of the school bell alerted the students, that class had ended. They all rushed out of their seats anxious to exit the room with Onyx being at the tail end of the line. Crush knew she was beautiful as a teenager, but for the first time she had seen Onyx in her body in a more beautiful way than before. She had walked right through Crush as if she was a ghost in the middle of the room. Onyx started trotting and smiling with school books pressed against her breasts, happy and harmful to the world. Crush heard the teacher call out to Onyx from across the room for her to stay back to have a word with her about her grades. Onyx joyfully walked over to the teachers' desk as the classroom door slammed shut behind the last student leaving. She answered yes to the teacher awaiting to hear what he had to say, when he grabbed her by her inner thigh in a sexual manner that made her freeze were she stood in shock by his actions.

Crush watched Onyx push the teacher's hand away in anger. There was a big poster covering the classroom door, so no one could see what was about to occur behind the walls of a school that teaches morals and values through the eyes of God. Onyx dropped her books to the floor, and slapped the teacher in his face with much force. He then grabbed Onyx roughly by her waist side, pushing his hands up her skirt, and forcing his fingers into her. The teacher was young and too strong for Onyx to fight. So she let him fondle her until he was satisfied. Crush watched with her mouth wide open as the teacher taunted Onyx on, how no one would believe a mentally challenged nigger girl. Crush could not stop the tears from rolling down her cheeks.

In the same second, the scene changed again before her eyes. Crush now found herself standing in a pile of horse shit. She stepped to the side, and began to rub the horse manure off her boots in dry hay. She was in someone's barn obviously. She looked around to see if Onyx was still present with her. No sign of Onyx. The barn was filled with horses in their separate quarters. She then realized it was her parent's farm, the one she grew to love in her childhood life. She put a smile on her face for a quick second, when she heard a muffled moan coming from the top level of the barn.

Crush patted one of the horses on the head in passing, as she made her way towards the wooden ladder leading up to the place where her parents had forbidden her to go when she was a teenager. Remembering her dead parent's request, she paused and thought if she should continue and go against their wishes. Then she heard the moan again. It sounded like someone was in pain. So she slowly climbed the ladder step by step, until her eyes became leveled to the floor view. She placed her right hand on the edge to boost herself up, when she felt a sticky wet substance on her palm. The hay stuck to her palm, like a fly caught on fly paper. She lifted the rest of herself up to get a better balance. Finally standing up fully, she then brushed the hay off her brown knitted sweater and her hand as well.

It was a bit dim at the top level of the barn, so she had to squint her eyes to get a good look at her hand. Thick red blood covered her whole entire palm. But the moans got louder as she realized they were coming from behind the large bales of hay stacked to the roof. She wiped the blood on her jeans as she crept around the bales to see what that moaning was. The more she turned the maze of bale; the buzzing of flies filled the air around her face. She had to brush them away, because there were so many. She paused as she focused her eyes on a large herd of flies covering what appeared to be a large piece of raw bloody meat pinned to one of the bales of hay. Shooing the flies, she realized it was a piece of human flesh. Still freshly cut and dripping with fresh blood as well. Quickly backing away, her feet slipped from under her, causing her to fall in another pile of hay, this time covered in pints of blood. Her back and cloths were drenched from head to toe.

Looking straight up, still lying on her back, she saw the school teacher tied to the roof's beam by rope, naked and skinned from his neck down. His stomach was slit wide open exposing his intestines and internal organs. His dick was hanging from a separate rope dangling directly in front of her face. Replaced in the spot where his decapitated penis should be, was a strap-on dildo, a black one. Blood drops dripped on her face as she was in awe witnessing the true horror of what Onyx was capable of doing. She began to scream at the top of her lungs. The more she screamed, the more blood covered her face from the teacher's body that was disfigured, and left to rot by the hands of Onyx.

Screaming and kicking on the floor, Crush felt two hands grab a large patch of her hair, and then drag her body from under the dripping blood. Onyx dressed in her Catholic school outfit pulled Crush by her head over to the ledge, as if she was lighter than a ragdoll. It was like Onyx had the strength of ten men when she picked Crush up by her throat and hung her weak body over the ledge in mid air. Kicking her legs with nothing but 18 feet to the bottom floor, Crush mumbled no as Onyx's grip got tighter and tighter cutting off her air supply. Looking in Onyx's eyes, she had to think quickly. She knew what had to be done. She started to remember it was all in her mind.

"This is over." She let herself fall from Onyx's tight grip looking into her eyes on the way down. She opened her eyes right when she hit the floor. Then the sound of banging on the bathroom door startled her for a second.

"Crush, open the fucking door! I have to take a serious shit! This isn't funny at all! Come on girl, stop playing!"

The sound of Brian's voice gave Crush a comfortable feeling to know she safely returned after pulling a crazy experiment like that. "Hold on Brian" she shouted at the bathroom door. "Don't get all crazy, I was taking a dump too." Crush ran over to the mirror to fix her frizzy hair do, when Onyx cast a reflection back at her, dressed in her Catholic school out-fit, and reached out and grabbed a hold of Crush's throat. Crush let out a screeching loud scream, and in a flash, Onyx was gone. Brian nearly kicked the doors of their hinges when he heard her scream so loud. He rushed inside displaying karate moves as if he was Jet-Li or Jackie Chan. She turned in his direction and began to laugh so hard, she had to grab her stomach from hurting.

"And what the hell were you going to do Brian? What kind of Kung-Fu bullshit was that?"

"Stop playing Crush, you know I get it popping up in here!"

"Yea, sure you're a killer."

"Whatever Crush, you had me there for a minute."

"Whatever you Dragon Lee Jones from Martin T.V show, all I know is that, you better fix my damn door!" Crush grabbed his cock on the way out laughing.

Walking down the hall on her way to the bedroom, she pressed her hand against her forehead processing what had just happened. She sat down on the bed to catch her breath when the house phone rang. She picked up the phone to the sound of music playing in the background.

"Hello? Hello, who is this?" there was the sound of someone giggling on the other end followed by a Click. The other person hung up the phone in her ear.

CHAPTER SIX:

"Double Trouble"

The sound of the Notorious Biggie Smalls CD "Life after Death" was loud and blearing in the air. "Somebody got to die/Let the gun shots blow.!" Asteria, one of the Twins, known as "The Twin Assassins" sat on a plush queen size bed at the Trump Towers Hotel, in a sexy Victoria's Secret V-string panties set. She was still giggling as she hung up the phone receiver to the hotel room.

"You are so crazy sis!" Leto replied to her sister walking by the bed holding in her hands two 9 mm G36 hand guns in her palms. She was also looking all sexy in her luxurious lace and streamlined mesh Victoria's hugging her curvy hips. She checked herself out in the mirror admiring her petite teenage shape, while Asteria continued to lip-sink the words to Notorious B.I.G. She took a deep breath and sighed, walked over to the bed and asked Asteria to help her pull the large Louie Vutton duffle bag from under the bed.

"I believe if you use enough muscle, you will achieve your goal." She said with a serious look in her eyes. Leto looked her back in the eyes and with one hand she pulled the bag from under the bed. She plunged it on the bed beside Asteria. Asteria reached over and patted Leto on the butt cheek with a smile. "That's what I'm talking about sis!" Leto then unzipped the big bag exposing the contents inside.

Guns! Guns! And more Guns; Four nickel plated Desert Eagle 45 chrome pistols, three Desert Eagle 50 caliber action express, long slide infrared beam pistols, six 9 mm G36 palm hand guns, and two MP5 Assault Rifles. She then unzipped the side pocket to the bag and in it was, C4 explosive putty with wires attached to small timers, and 50 boxes of assorted ammunition, and 20 clips fully loaded. Asteria still spread across the bed staring up at the ceiling, was making circles with a large bullet around the outer perimeters of her nipple. Leto tilted her head in her sister's direction and put a look on her face like a puppy would do when puzzled. "You are such a freak." She replied. They both burst out in laughter just like teenage girls do. What might seem cute to most teenagers was never cute to these young killers. They were never your average Home Coming Queen school girls. What they were taught growing up was how to kill without out remorse, how to live their lives without fear, without regard for the lives of others. They were born Assassins!

Ms. Crush Onyx was born September 12th 1969. Conception with the twins was in 1988, which made her 20 years old, during the time of Dr, Kenneth Korvach's crazy experimental sessions with "Onyx" running loose in society, killing and creating her new life. How does one personality control the body, while the other is suppressed?

Disorders in clinical research conducted by Sigmund Freud's teacher, the French Neurologist Jean Martin Charot; and collaborator, Austrian Physician Joseph Breuer (1842-1925). Dr. Korvach who was stimulated by their teachings and the demonstration of the Therapeutic Value of Hypnosis used the hypnotic state not for the purpose of suggestion, but to uncover painful and forgotten memories in his neurotic patients. By this technique, he helped his patients, but also observed clinically important causes of mental illness.

When Crush Onyx was placed in the private school and Estates of Korvach Clinical Institutes, Bloomington, Indianapolis at the age of six, by the time she was in her late teens, Korvach's experiments were way out of control. At the age of 19, Onyx in control of the body had escaped once more from behind the gates that surrounded the large Estate. In that first year of being loose in society, and Crush trapped in the far psyche, Onyx had given birth to beautiful twins. Onyx knew that Dr. Kenneth Korvach had fathered her children. Crush had lost her virginity to Brian, while Onyx lost hers to Korvach.

Onyx had made her way to London changing her identity several times in her travels. After the twins Asteria and Leto were born, immediately Onyx founded the underground Cult called "The Sandbox". The two members of this Cult called "the Sandbox" were two identical twin brothers she made her most prized personal bodyguards, "The Invisible Men". She called them that because their faces were always rapped up like mummies in white cloths. Their mother sexually abused them so much that they could not stand the sight of their own faces. Although these brothers were so beautiful in looks, they finally snapped and murdered her in the most gruesome way. Three years later, two more members were added; Victor Vegas, known as "Vanish", and Blake Wellington, known as "Pretty Face." Victor Vegas was an Ex C.I.A. Agent trained by the Government in Explosives, Weapons, and Tactical Assassinations. Victor was also trained in changing his complete identity at any given time using his surroundings. A real master at Passport, Drivers' License, and Identification alterations, A master at disappearing, which gave him the code name; Vanish! He had killed so many people throughout his missions that it drove him to be labeled Clinically Insane, and one of America's Top 5 most deadly men. "Pretty Face" Blake Wellington, was a master at finding people. Just like a blood hound dog, he could pick up their trail and find that person anywhere. Tabitha Black known as "Black Butterfly", was actually the baby of the cult, meaning the last to become a member. But the Twins in age are the youngest.

"Finally" The cell phone belonging to Asteria began to ring. She flipped the phone open with much anticipation.

"Are you girls ready?"

"Yes sir" As she snapped her fingers at Leto to write down their orders.

"The return of your mother Onyx has been long awaited. Her enemies have profited quite a bit since her absence. The Dragon Syndicate has made a mockery out of the Sandbox for years. They would never attempt to do so if they knew Onyx was still in control of that shell she has been placed in by Korvach. Being what may, she was prepared for her return. Her orders are precise to this date. How she knew these things are not of question. She is wise and powerful. What we accomplished before your birth was a mere walk in the park. We have changed the views of this pathetic society we live in today and their attempts to control our minds, our beliefs and our ways. We will strike a blow tonight that will let our enemies know we are back with vengeance."

Asteria rolled her eyes as Vanish continued.

"The head, Lee Chow and the thirteen members of their organization are having a birthday party for his twenty year old son, John Chow. It's being held upstairs in the penthouse. The whole entire floor is rented for his family. I know you and your sister are used to quick and deadly hits, and love to make an entrance before killing your marks, but tonight will be different. You are to use less action, and more skill to kill them all in one shot."

"Yes we understand Mr. Vanish. I'm guessing we have to place the C4 explosives in each room, including the party room without being caught. Sounds like a step up for me and my sister. I can assure you we are professionals at what we have been trained to do. So don't worry, we got this dude. We will party a bit, get our drinks on, and blow this joint. Get it? Blow this joint?"

"Yes I get it Asteria. Just obtain the goal!"

She giggled to herself. The silence was long and paused for a few seconds. The phone clicks in her ear.

"That man needs some ass, real bad. Anyway Leto, let's get our party on sis!" without hesitation, they sit and plan their attack.

The large conference room located at the penthouse floor, sits the six heads of one of the most powerful Chinese underground organizations, The Dragon Syndicate, also knows to the F.B.I. as the "Triads!" At the head chair, Mr. Lee Chow faces the large window looking down to Manhattan.

"The view is always amazing at night here. Although the Americans can't compete with China's beautiful landscapes, I have been doing business here in New York for twenty years, Los Angeles for ten, and Chicago for five. New York has always been the best."

The five members nod their heads in agreement.

"I think we can all agree that we have made it easy for our children to have a better life than the ones in China. Now they can give their children the same, and a good education. We have made Billions in profits through our businesses all over the world. It has now come the time to pass my business over to my First son." He spins his chair in his son's direction. "Son, it's time for you to take your place as head of our family, Are you ready for your destiny son?"

"Yes father, I am ready to be loyal, and dedicated to this family and the organization. I will take my place as head!"

Mr. Chow gets up from the table and walks away. He faces the window with his hands behind his back folded. In seconds the sound of pattering filled the silent conference room. A small Asian man comes running straight to Mr. Chow carrying two large cases. With one knee he bows and hands my Chow the cases without making eye contact. He takes the cases and waves the man away. He places them on the wooden table, pops them open and exposes two custom made swords, one with a Dragon engraved in the center, and the other with a large koi fish. Chow, with speed, grabs the swords and tosses one quickly to his son. The sound of steel against steel echo's the silent filled room. No one moves from their seats.

A battle between father and son is most important in the ceremonial transaction of leadership in the Triad organization. If the son cannot defeat the father in battle, then he is not fit to head the family. Still no words exchange in battle, just the sound of heavy breathing and grunts and moans of the battle. Minutes seem like days in the mind of young John Chow. He knows one false move can shatter 21 years of training for this moment. Discipline is the hardest part of this battle for him. His greatest demon is the discipline to kill, even if it's a family member. A sister, brother, even his own parents. Betrayal is the most deadly demon to kill. If he can kill someone who is disloyal, then that can cost him his own life as well.

John closes his eyes and slows down his breathing. With four swift and careful moves that his teacher did not show him, his father is disarmed and knocked to the ground on his back. Lee Chow opens his eyes to a hot and chipped blade to his throat. The room is silent for a few seconds. The other five members rise from their seats in an attempt to help. But with one hand, Lee stops them by a signal to pause. John bows down on one knee and mutters, "father".

"You are ready my son" John extends his arm to help his father rise. The members bow in the direction of John Chow, the new head of his family's dynasty.

"Let the celebration begin!" they all exit the room patting John on his back dressed in their thousand dollar suits.

Asteria calls for room service while Leto sets the timers on the C4 explosives. All weapons are loaded and placed neatly on the bed, ready to use. Leto was dressed in a Maids out-fit with a phony name tag. Asteria is in a two piece business suit, posing as a Hotel Manager also with a fake name tag. In all reality, the two bodies were neatly tucked in the closet. Room service is on time with a knock on the door. Asteria opens the door to let the Room Service Clerks wheel in two large carts with lots of food and silverware.

"Can you guys please wheel them in the back room" she says with a smile.

Both clerks are puzzled not knowing if she was truly a manager as she assisted them in wheeling the carts in. Their eyes got so wide when they saw so many guns on the bed. Two shots from a silencer in the back of their heads ended the confusion. Blood and brains everywhere, Leto is ruthless in assassination, and a killer without a conscious. Asteria takes a large bite from the Lobster under the silver platter. "I'm starving" then tosses it in the trash can. Leto cleans the platters off and places the C4 in place of the lovely food and puts the tops back on. They lift the cloths and place all the guns under to be covered. Leto grabs her baby's, two G36 9 mm pistols with silencers and places them in straps around her thighs under the skirt slip, when another knock on the door distracts

her? Both sisters pause for a second and squinted their eyes at each other and cocked the chambers back on their guns.

They were very discreet in getting the room, so that could only mean one thing? Someone else knew they were there. Asteria put the small hand gun back in its holster and reached under the cart and pulled out the MP5 fully loaded with infrared scope and mufflers on the tips for silent shots. Just as she pulled the safety lever, the door handle was blow open by a shot gun from the other side. Leto jetted to the left smoothly and hit the light switch while taking cover in the dark. Asteria darted to the right of the room rolling over the bed and hit the floor. In a flash, four Chinese men entered the room blazing Uzi's with silencers as well. The door was closed by the last man to enter. Shots rang out from all directions. In the dark, it looked like thousands of strobe lights in a club. Shells hit the floor; pillows were ripping to shreds as feathers filled the air.

"HOLY SHIT! Asteria! They know we're here, LETS ROCK MOTHER FUCKERS!"

"THIS SHIT IS NOT GOING TO BE EASY LETO!" as they shouted to each other, waiting for a pause to fire back.

"HOW THE FUCK DID THEY KNOW WE WERE HERE ASTERIA?"

"HOW THE FUCK DO I KNOW BITCH!" Asteria answered with a smile on her face.

The Chinese men maneuvered themselves behind the tables and desks as they reloaded their weapons.

"WELL LET'S KILL THESE MOTHER FUCKERS AND BLOW THIS SHIT UP!" Leto shouted standing up. She was swift with her aim letting off two single shots with her infrared beam, with direct hits into the foreheads of the two men, splattering their brains out their skulls. In that same moment a bullet found its way into Asteria's shoulder. The bullet made her skin sizzle like a melting piece of butter. "I'M HIT SIS, BUT IT WENT STRAIGHT THROUGH!" she fires back wildly hitting the two remaining men in their chest killing them instantly. They pause and scanned the area with their eyes to make sure the men were dead.

"SHIT, now my suit it ruined Leto. There is a traitor amongst us. The game changes a lot for us now, someone doesn't want us to come out of this one alive. Mom has been sold out to the Chinese."

"Well let's kill all these squinted eyed chinks and get mid-evil once we found out who the traitor is."

"It doesn't matter right now Leto. Grab the cart, leave the guns and rap this shit up. But wait a minute, I have an idea?"

A cleaning lady exits the elevator about to make her nightly clean-ups listening to her I-Pod bopping her head to the sounds of Salsa music. As she turns the corner, she sees a black cloud of smoke coming from under one of the doors. She screams "Ai Dios Mio!" and pulls the fire alarm. The loud alert caused frenzy. Visitors filling the hall with panic making their way to the nearest exit. Security guards spitting into their radio's telling everyone to be calm. Meanwhile on the top floor where the Chow Family gathered around the two elevator doors waiting patiently for hotel management to explain what was going on, was met with two food carts with roses and pretty trimmings. Mr. Chow's eyes could not squint any lower as he watched his bodyguard pull the carts off the elevator to make room for them to exit. Beep, beep, beep….BOOM!

Outside on the streets of Mid-town Manhattan, observers watched in horror and shook when the huge burst of flames and flying glass shot out the windows to the whole top level of the beautiful hotel. The blast was so powerful that car alarms went off at ground level. People ducked from the falling bricks and glass, and females screamed at the top of their lungs. Fire trucks made their way up the crowded street.

"My God Bill, do you see that. What the hell is going on?"

"I don't know Murphy? Let's just hope it's not another terrorist attack. All those people up there, it has to be at least a few hundred?"

Fully dressed, Bill and Murphy were the first firemen to reach the front doors to the hotel. The glass doors shattered as frantic people came pouring out like army ants on a food hunt screaming and crying. The pushing crowd was hard to control, not giving the two firemen a chance to enter the building. Police cars and sirens filled the street setting up barricades to keep the crowd in for statements and questioning. In the crowd two girls stood watching, observing and calm as hell.

"Now let's get back to our secret safe house and take care of my shoulder. We can't trust anybody right now sis. We need to get into that woman's head and get mom out so we can handle this shit."

"What do you have Asteria. A crack skull here in case of emergency hammer? That's not possible yet! Muah-ha-ha-ha, Muah-ha-ha-ha!"

"Why the hell are you laughing like that Leto?"

"I always like that Dr. Evil mad scientist, Austin Powers's movie."
Asteria stared at Leto for three seconds and began to laugh. "Muah-ha-ha-ha, Muah-ha-ha-ha!"

CHAPTER SEVEN:

"I LOVE NEW YORK"

10:00 pm, David Allgood, F.B.I. Tactical Unit Supervisor, paces around in his office on the phone trying to explain the shooting of Tabitha Black to his superiors. Candice and Michelle watched him send an angry glare through the glass doors to his office.

"Damn Candice. You would think we did him a favor by getting rid of a psycho killer like Black Butterfly!"

"Yeah Michelle, But we could have tried to get her to talk a little more about Crush Onyx and get info on how they knew each other?"

"Do you really think she would have told us anything we needed to know? These people live by a code. She wouldn't have told us shit!"

"But it was like she knew we were coming? She practically gave us a warning about what was to come. She looked me right in my fucking eyes and told me it's not over!" Agent Candice said with a huge puzzled look.

Michelle leaned back in her chair and sighed. She then pushed forward and placed her elbow on the desk looked Candice in her eyes. "Look, in the last past 48 hours we were shot at, almost blown to shit, found a picture with her and Crush Onyx, killed her, and damn near lost our jobs. You know what Candice?"

"What Michelle?" Candice answered.

"I love you. OK, not like that home girl, I don't do white girls. White rich guys, maybe, but I'm not a muffin muncher."

Candice opened her mouth wide open and laughed out loud.

"I love you too Michelle. So how do we ask Allgood for some personal time? Well, I know he would be glad to give me the time off. He made that perfectly clear!"

"Please girl, he's so mad I'm betting he'd pay for it out of his own pocket. Let's just tell his sorry ass we need it to relax from all the action. Plus you've been shot remember!"

"True dat–true dat!"

Candice said pounding her chest like a dude.

"Agent Blake, Agent Sums. Come in my office. NOW!"

Candice and Michelle grabbed their reports off the desk and gave each other a smile and proceeded to Allgood's office.

They entered Allgood's office without saying a word. He pointed at two chairs opposite of his seat indicating for them to have a seat. As Candice and Michelle took their seats, so did Allgood, behind his large oak wood desk. Allgood leaned back in his chair putting his hands folded on his lap. Anxiety filled the air.

"Please put your reports on my desk ladies!"

"Yes sir!" Candice and Michelle answered in unison. Allgood suddenly slammed one hand on the table hard as hell. Only Candice jerked her body to the loud bang.

"GOT DAMNIT Sums and Blake! I know you both think I'm being a complete fucking asshole, but there's a chain of command in the bureau! And believe me when I say they are bigger dicks than I can ever be. Now I'm sorry I came at you both harshly earlier, but you are the two best Agents I have that can do the shit you do!"

"Best Agents?" Michelle said looking at Candice with a puzzled look.

"Sums please close my blinds." Candice did so and returned to her seat.

"Yes I said it. Best Agents I have in this unit. Michelle, I knew your father very well. I'm deeply sorry he lost his life in the field. He was a good man and he would be proud of you today, but enough of that. There are two Agents who took over the Crush Onyx case after the Doctor Kenneth Korvach death. They both have been missing since last year. NO FUCKING LEADS AT ALL!"

"WHAT THE HELL!" Candice shouted out loud standing up out of her seat in anger.

"Sit your ass down Sums!"

"BUT, ALLGOOD"

"SIT THE FUCK DOWN Sums! That's an order!" Candice slowly sat back down. "Yes I know how you must feel. I'm still pissed off about how close you both came to catching this Crush Onyx character. I can't sleep sometimes myself knowing she's still out there, free. That's why I'm letting you both go back out there to get this crazy chic. Something doesn't sit right about Tabitha Blacks death? I also know about the picture too, Sums."

"You do sir?" Candice said.

"Yes! Nothing gets past me. But I can't see that evidence myself, it would compromise my involvement. Although it's against my better judgment, I'm letting you both do this on your own. If you are successful, you will both get full credit for the mission. I'm not sure why

I'm letting you both do this in the first place, other than for the fact that you both know her better than anyone else at the bureau."

"Yes sir, you have no idea how much this means to us!"

"Let me finish Sums! I have two other Agents out of the New York bureau that have been on the case as well. They also lost good friends and Agents dealing with this case. The four of you will team up when you arrive and dig up whatever you can to bring this case to a close. We also have an order of protection against us from the courts. That's why you have to be on the down low. Follow her, but do not, and I mean do not compromise the mission by jumping the gun!"

Michelle raised her hand as if she was still in high school. Allgood answered, "Are you fucking kidding me Blake?"

"Umm, sorry sir, we need umm, well you see, me and Candice, umm…"

"Yeah, you both need funds for this mission. I am giving you ten thousand stipends, that is more than enough. And please go shopping out there. You need to look as New York as possible. You both stick out like country bumpkins!"

"Thank you Sir. We will keep you on the open GPA line." Candice said with a great big smile on her face.

'*Now boarding gate seventeen*' echoed through the crowded Washington Dulles Airport, as people scurried along dragging their luggage. Candice and Michelle entered the doors to the airport carrying their travel bags as well. Agent Michelle pointed to the desk where their tickets should be. She let Candice know that it was alright for her to have a seat and watch their bags as she went to purchase the flight tickets. Candice was on her cell phone, so she nodded and continued to talk while Michelle went to do so.

The airport was loud, and the lines were long. Michelle was patient, but couldn't help herself from getting annoyed by the couple in front of her arguing over some bullshit vacation reservations that apparently weren't taken care of. She rolled her eyes and began to suck her teeth. The spoiled little dark skinned sister turned around and asked Agent Michelle if she had a problem with her conversation? She tried to keep her professional composure but the man she was with was too damn fine to be with this silly bitch, plus he seemed to be tired of his spoiled girl's attitude anyway. When the man turned his head in the direction that could become a very bad cat fight between his girlfriend and Michelle, the look on his face showed that Michelle was a beautiful and better candidate for this trip than the girlfriend accompanying him at this present time.

Michelle and that fine man exchanged quick eye to eye contact that clearly showed an attraction at first sight. Michelle couldn't hold it down then. She had to show her ass, so she opened her blazer exposing her fire arm. Her purpose was to show home girl she had more power.

"Excuse me Miss, I'm going to ask you to calm yourself down. Before you get yourself in trouble that you can't handle" Michelle said with attitude.

"So what are you some tough cop chic with a gun and a badge?

Candice turned her head to see how far Michelle was on the line when she observed the situation going down between the two of them.

"So what are you going to do? Shoot me now! I'm tired of bitches like you who think because you have a gun and a badge you can act all higher than us regular folk. Oh, and by the way, I'm just about to pass the bar exam with flying colors, so I know all my fucking rights."

Michelle chuckled sarcastically and took one step forward. Candice appeared out of nowhere grabbing her arm and whispered to Michelle in her ear reminding her that they were still on the case and to keep a leveled head at all times and not to draw attention to them. Michelle smiled and backed away from the woman.

"Yeah Candice Your right, I'm just a little tired. Maybe you should get the tickets. That bitch is pissing me the fuck off!"

She took the luggage from Candice and walked away to have a seat. As the long line got shorter and the couple in front of her purchased their traveling tickets, Candice approached the airport clerk.

"Two round trip tickets to New York please." Candice placed her credit card on the counter. "What will you be flying Miss?" The clerk asked. "Delta please" Candice answered.

Candice briefly took her attention away from the clerk, looking to her left through the crowded airport while the tickets were being processed. For a second she couldn't help notice that same short bald man across the floor was staring at Michelle. Then he diverted his attention and pretended to be reading a newspaper that covered most of his face. The man appeared to be a normal traveling businessman, but she noticed his reaction to their eye contact making him shift his position. Her F.B.I. instinct kicked into overdrive.

She began to scan the area he was standing in, pretending also not to realize he was in fact looking at Agent Michelle.

"That will be Delta flight 139, Terminal B, Gate 36, Miss Sums. You will have to pass security clearance for your weapon before getting on the shuttle bus to your flight."

Candice was distracted by the clerk. She turned to the clerk and said thank you while taking the tickets and her credit card off the counter. When she turned back around to walk away, she noticed that the bald headed man disappeared from the spot he was standing in. Her eyes shifted back and forth through the crowded airport trying to find the mysterious man. But there was no sign of him anywhere.

Maybe it's all in my head she thought to herself. She smiled and made her way back to where Michelle was sitting to find her exchanging business cards with that fine ass man whose girlfriend was being such a bitch. As she approached, the man was startled and began to shake Michelle's hand in a soft and gentle way making Michelle blush. He then hurried off back to his seat before his so called date would return. Michelle watched him walk away with a gleam in her eyes.

"Oh my God Candice he is so fine. To fine for her ass, fuck that shit. If a brother like that is feeling a sister like me, then let the games begin. Did you know he's also going to New York in two weeks for his business trip?"

"I would call you a slut, but I know you haven't been in a real relationship since- since- I don't think you ever been in a real relationship? So you are a slut!

Michelle slapped Candice on her shoulder and began to laugh out loud.

"Call me what you want, but plastic dicks and metal vibrators are not the real deal my friend."

Candice knew Michelle was too distracted to notice anything weird or to mention she thought they were being watched. So she laughed along with Michelle and kept her eyes shifting through the crowd. Something did not sit well in her gut about the mysterious man. Candice and Michelle made idle chat on their way to the security check point. Making their way through the crowded line, they flashed their F.B.I. badges and were directed by airport security to place their fire arms in a small box while waiting for clearance. Security insisted that they be driven privately. They did not have to be shuttled anywhere. They weren't regular civilians or commuters. Candice was hesitant, but Michelle was with that idea all the way. On the drive up to the plane, Candice's cell phone started to buzz. She answered it; it was Allgood on the line.

"Let me debrief you on what's going on. These are going to be your contacts in New York. The Agent's names are Antonio Delarosa, and get this, Mee Sun Young! Now Mee Sun Young went undercover as John Chow's so called love interest. John Chow is the son of Lee Chow, one of the six heads of the Dragon Syndicate known as the Triads! Real mean mother fuckers. She was pulled off the case and suspended because she fell too deep for the kid. So deep, she couldn't find it in her heart to bring him down. The only way she got out safely was because John was real big on the history that their families shared when they were children. You know the Asian culture, very disciplined in their ways."

Candice and Michelle made their way up the steps leading on to the plane. Candice was reminded by the flight attendant that all cell phone usage must end once the airlock doors were closed. Candice smiled and nodded in agreement.

"Allgood, I'm going to have to call you back on the private line. I will make the attendants aware that I'm with the bureau and need a line open."

"Call me back ASAP so I can finish debriefing you. This information is very vital to you and will be useful for you to know."

They made their way to their assigned seats. The flight was surely loud and crowded. Commuters in every isle, annoying, with their petty conversations. Michelle opened the storage bin doors over the seats and began to put the luggage in. Five seats back, the couple from the airport line was sitting ignoring each other. She tapped Candice to look over in their direction. Candice started to laugh softly, and then mumbled slut to Michelle.

Candice began to tell Michelle that Allgood was debriefing her on the contacts in New York, when a man in passing bumped into her and began to say he was sorry, when she realized who he was. It was the bald mysterious man from the airport. Once again she tried to convince herself that she was being paranoid and that her imagination was running wild again. She sat down next to Michelle who had this big ass grin on her face while trying to look inconspicuously at him five seats back.

"Wow Michelle. You are sweating the shit out of that man. What are you up to now?"

"Mmmm, I don't want to even say. I did have this one fantasy getting fucked in a plane bathroom before."

"Oh my god Michelle, it's not as comfortable as you think. The rooms are small as hell and my first time was horrible!"

"YOU FUCKING FREAK! I knew you was a slut too Candice. All you white girls are."

"Totally different Michelle, I was engaged to be married. He wasn't another woman's man. You're just crazy like that. But I love you though."

Michelle smiled while placing her laptop on the seat table preparing to go online after the plane took off. "Ladies and gentleman, the cabin doors are locked. Please turn off all electronic devices, fasten your seat belts and make sure trays are stored and seat is in an upright position. A flight attendant will be coming around to do one final check in preparation for takeoff."

Twenty minutes into flight the attendant made it clear for computers and all electrical devises to be used. Michelle opened her laptop and Candice picked up the phone located in the chair in front of her above the tray, with a laptop placed on her lap as well. Candice was connected to supervisor Allgood and began taking notes about her debriefing.

"As I was saying Sums, Mee Sun Young had just found out that the bodies identified at the hotel explosion in Manhattan were in fact the members of the dragon syndicate leaders. Including Lee Chow, the father of John Chow, but John Chow's body was not identified yet. New York's F.B.I. Bomb Squad believes that John Chow was not killed in the attack, although his name was on the roster."

"But what does any of this have to do with Crush Onyx sir?" Candice asked.

"Through other agencies and Intel evidence, Crush Onyx is somehow connected to the underground world as well. It has come to my knowledge recently through pulling some old ace cards, you know favors. Onyx, Crush's alto ego formed an underground cult called "The Sandbox." How many members are unknown. I was also told there might be a connection to a pair of young females whom call themselves "The Twin Assassins", it is also speculated that these girls are the offspring of Crush Onyx!"

"This fucking shit keeps getting better and better. Are you serious sir? Your telling me that not only is Crush Onyx a threat, but she recruited her own daughters?"

"Yes Candice. This case is becoming more and more of a headache. I was trying to put all the information together myself. So now you see why this case is so dangerous. You and Michelle can figure your approach when you meet up with Agents Delarosa and Young."

"Yes sir, will do. Thank you for the debriefing. I will call you in a few days after we're settled in our hotel in New York."

"Ok Sums, please be careful out there. Come back in one piece. No pun intended, just come back alive you two."
"Yes sir!"

Candice turned to Michelle with a serious look on her face. Michelle unplugged her laptop and turned her head facing the window and shaking it in disbelief. They both sat in their seats trying to keep calm and keep their composure. Keep from looking worried about all that has happened and what is to come. Cold chills ran up their spines, because they knew how much more dangerous the mission has now become. The Black Butterfly was dangerous. Crush Onyx, now Twin Assassins? How many more has Onyx recruited to bring horror and pain to innocent people in the world? So they sat and did not say a word the whole flight?

Arriving at JFK airport located in Queens, New York, departing from the plane, Michelle felt she had to break the silence by bursting out singing Frank Sanatra's New York anthem.

"I like to wake up; in a city that doesn't sleep-bada dada. Don't you just love New York Candice?" Candice smiled back and replied yes.

Moments later, walking through the airport dragging their roller luggage, Candice noticed, once again the mysterious bald headed man is following closely behind them in the crowd. That was enough of trying not to be paranoid. Then she whispered to Michelle in a calm and cool manner.

"Michelle, don't look back but we have been being followed ever since we left Virginia. He's a bald white male, about five foot six, a few people behind us. He's wearing a black blazer with grey slacks, brown shoes and reading specks."

"Ok Candice. Let's direct him towards the restroom area. If he is following us for sure, we would know."

They continued to act like they didn't notice him, but yet leading him to the restrooms. Just as suspected, he followed. The shuffle of the crowd made it hard for the bald headed man to get a clear view of both Agents actually entering the female bathroom. He then made his way closer to the area and waited for a few minutes while pretending to be in deep conversation on his cellular phone. He watched women enter and exit the restroom. He became fidgety while waiting to see if he could spot Michelle or Candice. Still no sign of them made the man take action by entering the female restroom. Before he could get half way through the door, he was grabbed by both arms and shoved into the doors, face first, with brute strength. The man fell to the floor with blood gushing out of his nose. Other females screamed and began to panic not knowing what was going on. Michelle and Candice flashed their badges and pointed their weapons at the man on the floor.

"F.B.I.! Everybody out of the bathroom, NOW!" Candice shouted. As the restroom cleared Michelle places her fire arm on the back of the man's head as she kneeled on his back while he was face down on the floor.

"Who the fuck are you asshole?" Michelle asked.

"If you would be so kind to go inside my jacket pocket, there you will find my identification young madam." He said calmly with a British accent.

Michelle reached inside his pocket quickly and retrieved a wallet that displayed a badge that identified him as being British Intelligence.

"British Intelligence? Why didn't you identify yourself to us in the first place damn it! You could have prevented all this drama Mr. Hemington."

"Charles Hemington- Agent Blake, With all due respect to your bureau, my superiors insist I do not get involved with the U.S investigations about Dr. Kenneth Korvach's death or works with the young lady named Crush Onyx. You see, I work out of the London science department for abnormal formalities in the human brain that cause patients their sense to distinguish right from wrong, logical from illogical thinking. I can explain more in detail, but I do not believe this is the correct place to do so Agents Blake and Sums."

Leaving the women's restroom area, they found themselves a couple of seats at one of the airport's cafés. Candice and Michelle sitting opposite of Agent Hemington, they began to sip on some hot coffee, while he sipped on some imported tea from London. "He must not like American tea." Michelle whispered to Candice.

Hemington continued.

"Miss Crush Onyx has left me and the science department baffled in her astonishing behavior to be two complete separate personalities, and be able to interact with one another. I have researched some of Korvach's work files. I had to break the rules in order to get my hands on those personal documents. I had someone on the inside of the Korvach Estates when Crush was just a teenager. I was suspicious about him for as long as I can remember."

"If you don't mind me asking, Mr. Hemington, I need you to back up for a minute. What do you mean by Crush interacting with her other personality Onyx? Are you saying that Crush can talk to Onyx inside her head? So that means…"

"Yes Michelle. I know where you are going with this. That means that she has been set free based on falsified medical opinions supplied by Korvach to the courts."

"So what makes you seek our help?"

Candice sits and listens while sipping on her hot cup of coffee, waiting for him to answer Michelle's question.

"It's no mystery to any law enforcement around the world that you two have been the lead detectives on her case since the beginning. We who follow Serial Killings have been amazed at how close you have come to capturing Onyx, and then Korvach pulled that ridiculous stunt that freed her, and made Miss Candice look foolish all over the world."

"Thanks for the reminder." Candice said with a slight sarcastic tone in her voice.

"Pardon me Miss Sums, I did not intend to insult you. It was amazing work on your behalf." He begins to cough. "Excuse me; I was saying that after all the work you have done…'

Hemington begins to cough harder and harder when blood began to poor from his nose and mouth causing Michelle and Candice to jump up in confusion. They both began to panic calling for medical assistance to a nearby waiter.

"Call 911." Candice screamed again, at the waiter, as Hemington fell to the floor trying to loosen his tie to breathe.

"In my bag… there's a disc with documents I… I copied for you to… to…

"Just breathe Hemington, just be calm. Help is on the way." Candice replied frantically.

"I believe… I have been poisoned… there's someone here… who must have followed us… as well… I suspected Korvach was not working alone… I… I…"

Michelle searched the bag for the disc undetected before any medical personnel came.

"Hemington! Hemington!" Candice repeated while watching him die a slow death in her arms.

Hours later, Michelle and Candice sat in the Airport's security office going over what had happened with the New York police department and debriefing there superior Allgood as well via a phone conversation. The London Intelligence department arrived to take Agent Hemington's body back to his family and did not want to know why or what he was doing there. Their attitude was very clear that they did not like the fact that they lost one of their best agents in the U.S. without proper correspondence. Michelle and Candice were released immediately after London's Intelligence finished their business with them and the airport.

Walking to the exit doors, they were met by Agents Antonio Delarosa and Mee Sun Young. Standing there with their New York attitudes, hands in pockets, and shaking their heads at each other smiling. Antonio was a handsome Hispanic, tall with bushy eyebrows and slick faded haircut. His heavy "Antonio Banderas" accent, he introduced himself. It made him sound sexy and suave.

"Ello Michelle and Candice, I am agent Antonio. Welcome to New Jork." He grabbed both their hands and planted a soft kiss on each one. Agent Mee Sun Young slapped his hand down from theirs as she sucked her teeth at Antonio and punched him on the arm.

"Anyway, Hello Michelle, Candice, sorry about that macho bullshit he be trying to pull with every woman he thinks will fall for that shit." Mee Sun Yung had no Asian accent at all. She was straight New York from birth actually from the hood of Flushing Queens. She was short with long silky black hair that she kept up in a pony tail. She was also beautiful with strong Asian features.

"You can call me Mimi, or Young. Yes my name is crazy and I lived with it all my life, so it's ok to laugh, for now." She said shrugging her shoulders.

"Yea, I really don't use my accent that much either. I just love the stereotype cast of Hispanic men." Antonio laughed after his statement.

"So I see we are going to get along just fine as a team. Drama follows you too I see. What was that all about anyway?" Mimi asked.

"Well it's very nice to know you're not a couple of suits, and wear your badges up your asses. Me and Candice can tell you little on that, because we only knew the man for about two hours before he was poisoned." Michelle replied.

"Poisoned?" Antonio questioned.

"Yes. I think you should also know we, are being watched; someone poisoned him as soon as we arrived here in N.Y. at the airport. I think we should be very careful. It could have been one of us, but they did not want him to continue informing us about Dr. Kenneth Korvach." Michelle stated.

"Wow this is going to be a long investigation. Dangerous and full of surprises too. Well let's get you both to your hotel and get a good night's rest so we can start our mission to close the case on Crush Onyx for sure."

"That I agree. Well we have two GMC trucks waiting outside, one for you two, for your stay. I'm sure you ladies want to get around and see the sights before we go to work."

"Oh hell yeah Mimi, I'm so ready to go get some new gear form 34th Street. Girl we have a little New York flavor down south, but not all the real good shit like y'all." Michelle said with a serious southern accent.

As Young passed Candice the keys to their ride, she walked away and told them to follow them and please keep up. Sitting in the truck, Michelle looked at Candice waving the disc from Hemington, but she did not want to say anything out loud in fear that the truck might be wired with listening equipment. Candice gave a nod back and turned on the truck radio. The station was already set to Hot 97, one of the hottest New York Hip-Hop and R&B stations to listen too if you were in the City. Following Antonio and Mimi through mid-town, they pulled up to the valet parking at the Marriott Hotel on 47th and Broadway a few blocks down from 42nd Street Times Square. Michelle and Candice were so amazed at all the bright lights. They wanted to see it all right away. However, they knew that unpacking and getting settled in was necessary. Antonio helped the valet get their luggage while Young walked them to the front desk to check in.

"I really hope we can see the city like I want to." Michelle said as she received her door card to the room.

"I'm sure we will. But let's get settled and go over our files first."

"Yea, that sounds about right. Antonio and I already have the base camp set up on the 20th floor. We can start debriefing early tomorrow morning. Now I am heading home to get some rest. Enjoy the luxury." Agent Young gave them both a handshake and walked back towards Antonio who was patiently waiting in the truck outside.

Entering their room, Michelle immediately dropped her luggage in the middle of the floor and plopped on the bed letting out a sigh of relief, while Candice neatly placed her bag in the nearby closet at the door entrance. Michelle laid back on the bed and gazed at the ceiling, brushing her hands across the soft plush pillows. Candice took her blazer off and placed it on the chair at the desk where she pulled her laptop out of a separate bag and placed it on top. She asked Michelle to give her the disc that Hemington had given them before he died. Michelle sighed again and told her it was in her coat pocket and to get it herself. She was too comfortable to get up. Candice sucked her teeth, got up, got the disc and placed it in the hard drive of her computer.

TITLE: Regional Neurologist

SOURCE: Grand Rounds Presentation, Dept. of Neurology

DATE: April 17, 1991

RESIDENT PHYSICIAN: Charles Hemington, MD

FACULTY PHYSICIAN: Mitchelle M., MD

DOCUMENT FILE: #107

CASE SUBJECT: Crush Onyx

DATE: 4/17/75

Time: 6:45 pm

I have just induced Subject Zero with neutron inhibitor 67. Subject shows reaction to serum in 6.3 seconds once distributed throughout the blood stream. Personality #2 is suppressed and stays dormant in far psyche. Personality #1 has no recollection of transformation in body. Although I have successfully designed a serum to separate the split personalities, and keep them apart, I believe there can possibly be a side effect. For a moment, it appeared that both personalities had intertwined with one another, causing confusion in the mind. Nevertheless, the observation was not confirmed, so I will continue testing on Subject Zero until further development reveals itself in my experiments.

DOCUMENT FILE: #108
CASE SUBJECT: Brian Century
DATE: 8/24/87
Time: 2:32 am

Subject 6 cannot detect serum MC2 and has been successfully introduced to Subject by combining with liquid, distilled water preferred. Subject 6 is completely under mind control and unable to break free of my orders...

Candice sat there and continued to read over thirty case studies from Dr. Kenneth Korvach' files found on the stolen hard drive disc.

With her mouth wide open, still amazed at the ten names that were documented, Candice knew that Crush Onyx was just the first of many more sick experiments that Korvach had tested on in his career of being a neurologist/scientist. She pushed herself from the desk with force and excitement rushing to the bed where Michelle had fallen fast asleep with her cloths still on. While Candice was kicking the bed, Michelle woke up in frenzy, confused from the abrupt shaking of her leg.

"GET THE FUCK UP MICHELLE!"
"What the hell Candice?"

"You have to read this shit. We are in deeper than we ever been. I cannot believe how stupid I was five years ago not to know better. I always had the feeling that Korvach was never working alone in this shit. I'm telling you, this mother fucker probably has a whole army of people under some fucking brain experimental shit!"

Michelle yawned and walked over to the computer as Candice pushed her shoulders and guided her to sit and read.

"OK Candice Damn!" Michelle started to read from the first case file. The same one Candice started on from the opening of the documents. Just from the first couple of sentences, Michelle's eyes began to widen with every word read from then on. By the time she was finished with Crush's case study, she was in awe. They both looked at each other, with smiles on their faces, and in unison said…

"OH SHIT!"…

CHAPTER EIGHT:

"This Won't Hurt A Bit"

Effects of anesthesia

Hemodynamic changes consisting of hypertension, hypotension, or bradycardia are commonly seen in patients undergoing carotid endarterectomy. It is a potentially serious clinical problem that may increase mortality rates or incidence of neurologic deficits. The frequency of hemodynamic alterations has been believed to be related to the proximity of the carotid sinus baroreceptor to the endarterectomized region. Consequently, intraoperative (1) or postoperative (3) injection of local anesthetics into the carotid body have been recommended to help offset this compensatory mechanism.

Crush put the phone down and shrugged her shoulders as if it was not important that someone called her and hung up. She snuggled herself up against Brian while he was fast asleep, and began to think about Dr. Sanchez and her offer to schedule her for a counseling session. Crush knew the dangers of embarking on such a challenged endeavor with Dr. Sanchez exploring and allowing her curiosities to get the best of her profession dealing with Onyx. Sanchez has no fucking clue on what hell on earth is, if she was to unleash Onyx. Still, Crush wanted answers. Answers to what has been presented before her in the last 72 hours. As her eyes got heavier, opening and closing slowly with every blink, she just gazed at the vase on her dresser filled with fresh wild orchids that Brian had purchased the day before while waiting for her return. She gazed as if she was not looking directly at them, but right through them. Falling into a slow and deep sleep.

The time that Crush woke up did not matter to her. Whether it was 3 hours, or a full 10 hours of sleep, she was just feeling good about getting a good rest and start a new day. Brian was no longer beside her as she reached over eager to hug him. She lifted herself up and wrapped the sheet around her perfectly shaped naked body. She grunted as she dragged her legs off the bed planting her feet on the cold wood floor. Taking her left hand and placing it on her forehead pulling her loose hair from in front of her face so she can see down the hallway clearly. She leaned her neck slightly to the left still looking down the hallway, and realized that it was silent and still throughout the house. Meaning, Brian was not in the condominium at all. Looking to the left, then to the right, she smirked her lips to the side and sighed. Getting up and dragging her white sheet across the floor, holding it tightly under her arm pits, covering her perky nipples, she walked herself to the kitchen and proceeded to search her cupboard for her expensive and imported coffee grounds to put in the coffee maker.

Crush fumbled around with dishes from the dishwasher while waiting for the coffee to be done. After doing so, she arched her back, with her ass in an upright position leaning her elbows on the counter. Her ass looked so fluffy and soft covered with that white sheet. The sound of the coffee being ready snapped her out of a 15 second daze still thinking about why Brian didn't tell her he was leaving. He normally wakes her. Even if it was 3 am, his soft nudge to make her aware that he was leaving, had become repetitive. Taking a sip of the coffee, she snickered while swallowing, as she remembered one of her favorite movie scenes with Samuel L. Jackson, John Travolta, and Quentin Tarantino in the movie "Pulp Fiction". The scene was when Samuel was saying how good Quentin's coffee was while trying to smooth him over as he drove to his house with a dead body in the trunk. Quentin replied to Samuel; "I know it's fucking good coffee, because I buy the best fucking coffee! But that's not why you're here is it? It's the dead nigga in my garage!" Crush shook her head from side to side still laughing. The phone began to ring. The sound took her away from that thought. Answering the phone in a businesslike manner;

"Hello?"

"Hello Ms. Onyx. This is Dr. Sanchez from the hospital?"

"Oh hello Dr. Sanchez. How are you?"

"I'm doing great Crush. I was hoping you considered my offer to help you with....well you know. I rather not discuss that over this open line, I rather do it one on one. Is that ok with you?"

"Umm....you know what...sure."

"That would be great." Sanchez said with a high-pitched voice.

"What time should we schedule Dr. Sanchez?"

"Well can you call me on my cell phone?"

"Sure, let me get a pen....Ok, what is it?"

"1-347-555-6454, take a minute then call me Ms. Onyx"

"Sanchez, I rather you call me by first name please."

"Oh....ok Crush. Then I guess we can be on first name basis from here on in, so call me Karen."

"Ok Karen." Crush smiled and hung up.

Crush dialed Karen back.

"So Crush, we can have a session tonight after hours if that's ok with you."

"Sure Karen, what's a good time to come and see you? My day is empty. My boyfriend left me without saying goodbye. You know how that goes girl.......Oops, I'm sorry Karen. I just talk to my girlfriends like that. Sorry if I got over comfortable?"

"Mija, porfavor no te preoccupes." as Karen giggles over the line.

"What did you say?" Crush asked in a high pitched girly voice, as she giggled too.

"I said, girl please, don't worry about it, it's no big deal".

Crush and Karen both laughed together as it seemed their relationship was building. They said their goodbyes, and hung up!

8:00 pm displayed on the clock in Crushes Hummer as she parked her truck in the parking lot at Mount Sinai Hospital. The rain was beating down hard on her windshield as she gathered her belongings to exit her truck for her secret therapy session with Dr. Karen. The parking lot was dark and empty with only a few cars remaining in the lot that belonged to the night shift staff, mostly nurses.

Crush made her way to the automatic opening glass doors that made that silent sound as they slid opened. As she made her way up the hallway, two young black orderlies paused their conversation, as they whispered to each other while she was walking passed them. She could hear them both say at the same time, DAMN! That woman is fucking fine. They both smiled at her giving her respect not to act unprofessional, although she did hear the F word. She looked back and smiled and replied back. "You are both kind of cute too" and continue to put just a little more switch in her hips.

As she finally made it to the front desk, a West Indian nurse by the name of Clare asked crush her name and what was the nature of her visit. Crush told her she was there to see Dr. Karen Sanchez. Clare made a call to Karen's line alerting her that Crush was there to see her.

"She will be right here in a moment Ms. Onyx" Clare said with a strong accent.

"Thank you" Crush replied back with a smile.

The front desk area was slightly dim, because the patient visiting hours were over, and the night nurses have the option to turn down all the bright lights in their unit if the area is empty and most of the patients are resting. They are probably sedated from the medications and pain killers given to them while they heal from their surgeries.

Crush walked over to a soft leather couch placed against a wall midway in the hall. She took a seat and started to twiddle her thumbs, put a smirk on her face as she gazed at two nurses across from the front desk talking about how they were under paid for all the shit they have to deal with. She shook her head and smiled to herself. A few minutes went by and she could see Karen down the hall entering and then exiting room after rooms checking on her patients making sure their charts were correct. Finally Karen was close enough to greet her and tell her to follow her. She shook her hand with a smile.

"Crush I am so pleased that you would give me the chance to have this session with you".

"Sure Karen, but how much is this gonna cost a sister?" Crush asked as she smiled walking up the hall with Karen.

"Oh Please Crush. I told you this is on my time girl."

"I hope this will help me figure out why I passed out for no reason?"

"Well Crush, there is never no reason for passing out. I'm sure we can find reasons to the why. With a lot or little work, we both want answers."

"Well Karen, I'm sure you know about my history and I'm wondering why you would be this concerned to help me."

"It's my sworn Oath to............."

Crush cut Karen short from finishing her sentence.

"Oh Please, if we are going to do this, please leave all that text book shit out. I don't need you to act the part Karen. I just felt you were sincere in your concern to help me just because."

Karen stopped short in her tracks, let out a soft sigh.

"You are right Crush, I will leave all the bullshit out dealing with you. I just have to cover my back, and make sure you don't flip it on me. I have a lot to lose. I could lose my job behind doing this without proper consent. I have a lavish shoe buying habit so I can't lose this job. I don't want to go back to buying Payless flip-flops!"

Crush burst out into a hard laughter after Karen said what she said with a serious face.

"Oh my God Karen, you meant that shit Huh? But I hear ya girl. I can't imagine not being able to buy my Jimmy Chu's."

"Shoot.......I hear that girl. What size do you wear?" Karen said looking at Crush's feet laughing.

After they bonded on the elevator to the top floor, exiting, Crush looked around and saw a whole new side to the Hospital that she never saw before. It was something straight out of that TV show "Grey's Anatomy" with plush carpet, and brown expensive leather couches with fancy end tables and pretty lamps on each one. The atmosphere was so comfortable; it looked like a loft apartment with all the trimmings.

"Is this your office Karen?"

"Yup. Listen girl, I say it was the Ph.D. that paid for all this. That paper is worth all this girl."

"It's cute though" Crush replied looking like....Only if Karen knew that she was worth a couple of Hundred Million anyway, and her Hotel rooms make this floor look like a normal waiting area at the Airport.

"Cute?"

"Yea cute"

Crush couldn't hold it anymore. She had to let it be known that she was not your stereotypical black woman from the Hood who makes less than a Doctor that has a flashy Loft office.

"I mean, it's nice. Well I do know expensive Luxury living. My parents left me a few Million from the Dairy Farms they owned before they passed away. Yea, I'm a trust fund baby. Call it what you want."

Karen blinked her eyes twice with a dead look on her face.

"Millions? Damn, maybe I should charge you then." Karen laughed as she sat behind her desk taking off her lab coat to get comfortable. "You can sit down on the couch for a minute. I have to put some paper work together."

Crush sat down and started to look at all the Degrees covering the walls over her desk and throughout the room. She was impressed that a Hispanic woman achieved such knowledge, and also killed the American taboo that minority can't make it because we are destine for failure. Crush noticed the nice glass vase, or it appeared to be a vase, when in fact it was filled with water to drink. She grabbed a glass and pored herself some water.

"I love this glass water pitcher Karen". She wanted to break the silence after she made that comment about having money.

"Oh thank you. It was a gift from this male nurse who wants to get inside my pants. He's cute, but I don't see us getting into sex like that. Plus I don't mix my job with sex. All I need is for him to be all over me, hovering over my shoulder, following me all through the Hospital getting jealous and causing problems. Shit like that!"

"I hear that girl and I'm sure you have other reasons why also. Is he short too?"
"How did you know? I have a height requirement girl."
"And does he think he's the Hospital Pimp?"
"DAMN Crush! Did you date him before?"

They began to laugh out loud at each other. The only thing they didn't do was give each other a high five.

"No, but it tells its own story Karen. I can understand."
"Ok. Now let's talk serious business sweetie."

Karen made her way to the couch and sat down beside Crush putting her hand on her lap. She told Crush everything that was about to happen. She explained that she would have to be put under a heavy anesthesia so she can search for some things from her past that might help. She also told her the rules to this session, and that she can stop when and if she feels it's getting to deep for Crush. Crush sat there and put a look on her face that showed complete fear.

"What's wrong Crush?"

"I don't think this is a good idea for us to do this."

"I thought you wanted answers and I'm right here in the room with you. It's just me and you. No one is going to hurt you."

"I'm not worried about me Karen. It's you who I'm worried about."

"Why would you worry about me?"

"I don't think you will agree if I tell you. I know this is where I should be able to tell all, but there are guidelines that you must follow as your oath states Karen."

"Well I'm very aware of who you are Crush. I won't lie to you. I am just as afraid as you are. I know about Dr. Kenneth Korvach. I know about your alter ego and split personality. I also know a little on how you should...or should I say...she is well locked away in your psyche. There shouldn't be much to worry about. She can't hurt anyone now....right?

"WRONG! I....I....still talk to her. She and I have been communicating full conversations for years now. She can't come out in physical form, or take control over my body, but she....she feels what I feel and tells me. That's why I need answers Karen. HOW....HOW is this possible?"

Dr. Karen Sanchez could not keep her professional composure on that one. Her eyes widened, her mouth opened, and she pulled her hand quickly back off Crush's lap and sat back so hard that you could hear the leather crumple and make that loud squeaky sound. She closed her mouth and you could also hear her swallow a gulp of spit that sounded like it weighed a ton.

The room was silent for a few seconds. Feeling like a complete idiot for saying that, Crush could not help but to react by getting up and making her way to the door in a quick rush to leave. Karen got up fast and softly grabbed Crush by her arm in an attempt to prevent her from leaving.

"CRUSH...Wait. I didn't mean to make you feel that way. It just took me by surprise. That's all."

Crush put her head down looking away from Karen, not wanting to look her in her eyes. She let out a soft sigh and grabbed Karen's hand and they made their way back to sit down on the couch.

"I know its crazy Karen. That's why I feel so alone on all this bullshit!"

"I understand how you must feel, confused and scared at the same time. But that's why we are here to find the answers."

Crush continued to tell Karen everything that happened from the parking lot, to how she winded up on her Hospital bed. Karen listened as

Crush told her about what Onyx had showed her on their mental journey from the past to the present. Karen sat there and was in awe and amazement as she could not believe that this could be happening. The conversation alone was two hours long. After Crush finished, they both needed a drink. And I'm not talking a glass of water either. Karen got up and found her stash of Bacardi Rum in her secret drawer. She told Crush she could not drink heavy because she still had to be put under. Crush agreed and let Karen filter what she had heard.

"Wow....well....ummm...ok. Let's take a minute and get to it then."

"Are you sure we should do this Karen?"

"I don't know Crush, but we can't sit back and let this consume you. I don't know about the other issues like your children and........"

"THEY ARE NOT MY CHILDREN! THEY'RE HER CHILDREN!" Crush said, in an angry tone, to Karen. "I'm sorry Karen. I just can't believe this shit is real!"

"It's ok Crush. I'm going to do everything possible to help you put your life in order. I can't promise anything, but I can damn sure be here every step with you. I give you my word, as your friend, I won't leave you Crush."

"Thank you that means a lot to me."

"Now Crush we have to start the first process. I need you to get as comfortable as possible on the couch. I'm going to give you something to relax."

Crush did as Karen said. She took off her shoes, laid back, and took a deep breath. Karen walked back to her desk and got the dosage of anesthesia to put Crush under. She dimmed the lamps to a soothing setting. She pulled Crushes sleeve up and tied the rubber around her bicep, and began to administer the anesthesia through her vein. Finishing that, she began to talk to Crush in a quiet soft tone.

"I'm going to count backwards from five Crush. I need you to go to the place where you think you can find one answer to a question. Don't try to go everywhere in one session, you will only confuse yourself. Remember you are in control......you are in control...control."

Crush could hear Karen's voice fade out as she wanted to go to one place, but winded up in a place that was not familiar to her....but to Onyx? There she was once again in the midst of images swirling around her as if she was in the middle of a hurricane of Onyx's past events. Then she realized that she was not in a room and there was no ground under her feet. Just as if she was standing on nothing but air. She stared for a few seconds, but was use to this all so well. So she began to walk forward into the Hurricane of images flashing before her. The voices and whispers echoed in and out, some familiar, some not. She could hear Dr. Kenneth Korvach's voice whispering close to her ear. She paused and tried to listen harder. She screamed out to him. "Korvach! Korvach! CAN YOU HEAR ME? IT'S CRUSH!...I NEED TO SEE YOU!....CAN YOU HEAR ME!"....no reply, just whispers, nothing she could understand.

Crush began to get annoyed. She began to give up. She turned back, wanting to wake up. She finally heard Karen call to her in a soft voice.... "Crushhh...Crush I'm right here with you, can you hear me Crushh?"...Karen's voice had a three time reverb sound effect as if it repeated itself overlapping one another. She answered back to Karen. "Yesssss." not knowing she was actually answering Karen on the couch. "Gooooodddd, I'mm Righhttt hereee Crushhh. Whereee areee youuuu?......." Crush couldn't answer her back because she was not sure if she was anywhere at all.

Then she blinked in her state of sedation. In one world she was on a couch. In the other, she was back at the Barn, at her parent's dairy farm. She froze and held her breath, trying to get a grip because the last time she was there, Onyx had her by the throat choking the fucking life out of her. She was standing in the same spot where Onyx had dropped her at in the last encounter. The soft warm breeze came through the barn scenting her nose with that old horse and hay aroma. The sun was brightly shining through the cracks of wood that held the barn together. To her left, in the stable, was her horse. Mr. Fuzzy was her name for him. She smiled and walked over to Mr. Fuzzy and began to brush her fingers through his mane and patted him on his forehead. She grabbed some loose hay off the bale that was placed next to the door that caged him in.

She began to feed him. He was just like she had remembered, so beautifully dark brown, with a white spot in the center of his forehead. Mr. Fuzzy was just the same as he always was, knowing his master, and enjoying her touch, letting her know, he remembered her as well. He seemed to stare Crush right in her eyes, as if he was asking her...'where have you been?' She continued to enjoy the moment not looking or paying any attention to what was behind her.

She looked up and shouted out to Karen. "CAN YOU HEAR ME? ARE YOU STILL THERE KAREN?" She heard Karen reply back in the distance. "Yes, what do you see Crush?" She answered back. "I'm home again. I'm in the barn with Mr. Fuzzy". Karen answered back, "That's good crush. Is that where you want to be Crush?" Crush looked around left to right, patted Mr. fuzzy, and began to walk out the barn. The sun was too bright for her eyes. So she put one hand up blocking the sun giving her face some shade to see the house. She began to walk towards her house with slow and carful steps. At least it appeared that she was moving slower than regular pace. Everything had a slow sway to its movements. The trees seemed to have a calm swaying dance to them as the winds blew softly through its branches. But then she looked up in the sky and to see the clouds were moving real fast? Like a film on fast forward. While on the ground everything moved in slow motion. She took a deep breath and continued to make her way to the porch of her house. There was an old rocking chair on the porch that her grandmother had passed down to her mother; it's been in the family for years. It was rocking back and forth from the warm winds blowing. The sound of that old creaking wood gave crush a real feeling of home. She walked up the three steps onto the porch looking from left to right again. She noticed the window overlooking the porch was wide open, with a hot apple pie cooling on the window pane. The dry brown leaves swirled in a circular motion over her feet and across the deck to the porch. She could smell the wonderful aroma of apples dipped in a sugary scent and the baked crust gave the finishing touches on it all.

Crush heard a voice? It was her mother's soft spoken tone coming from behind the opposite side of the double thick, wooden French doors that allowed visitors to enter. Crush rushed to open the doors to see her mother once again. The doors were locked and she could not enter. She then heard Karen's voice again in the far distance. "Crushh....where are you noww?".......Crush answered. "I'm on my porch. I can hear my mother calling for me to come in, but the door is locked.".....Karen's voice answered back... "Rememberrrr...yyou are in controlll Crush. If you wannttt to enterr, you cannn." Crush took a deep breath again, and whispered out in the direction of the doors. "Open" and without a second passing, both doors opened slow and wide allowing Crush to enter. A strong gust of wind came rushing out, blowing her long hair to flap upward as she entered. The smile on Crush's face expressed much joy, That her eyes watered as she found herself trying to run fast around every corner to find the kitchen where her and her mother would bake pies, and her mother would tell her stories about her culture and past relatives, and how they came to owning the dairy farm from a great, great grandparent that was a slave there. Her slave master loved her so dearly that when she died, she left all her land to her slave, and not her family.

Crush finally found her way to the kitchen. It was just as she remembered; the oak wood round dining table with twelve chairs neatly placed underneath, the table with a beautiful China dish set placed in order, matching glasses and coffee mugs, wine glasses that sat at each corner of the plate set, cloth napkins that matched the table sheet, the handmade marble topped center piece in the middle of the kitchen, with pot and utensil rack hanging down low from the high ceiling, and black and white checkered marbled tile floors. She was filled with so much joy, she turned towards the direction where the over was, and there she was. Standing there with her hands neatly placed in the pockets of her cooking jacket, her long hair in a high pony tail, just like Crush would wear it today, looking as beautiful as Crush did. Her mother's skin was so beautifully bronzed. Her shape was still as sexy as if she was still 20 years old, in her prime. Crushes mother almost resembled Iman the super model.

Crush whispered.........."Momma?......."

Her mother answered softly back, "Yes baby, you made it home. I missed so much my darling. We have so much catching up to do darling,"

Crush's put her arms out and walked over to her mother and gave her a hug and squeezed her so tightly with joy. Her eye burst into tears as she snuggled up under her mother's chin. Crush had yearned for her mother's touch ever so badly. Her mother's warm heart beat soothed her soul. They both stood there holding each other for dear life. Her mother's smile was so wide from ear to ear, her pearly white teeth could brighten up the sky. Her mother placed Crush's face in the palms of her hands and stared into her watery eyes.

"I waited here for you. I knew you would return. I couldn't leave this earth without telling you what I needed to tell you about.......about.......well baby, you know who." "Yes mother, I know. I don't know what to do. Why mother? Why couldn't you tell me about Onyx?"

"You were too young baby to understand what was happing with you. I hope you can ever forgive me. Me and your father tried everything to help you. He died an unhappy father from the guilt. He couldn't live know what was inside you. He blamed himself for many things that she did but it was nothing we could do. So we found Dr. Korvach, and placed you in his care."

"He's a very bad man momma. I saw what he did to me......to her....I mean....I don't even know what the hell I am anymore momma."

"Baby, you are who you are in spirit and in your heart. What she is, is a test from God. I know you might not want to hear that but you will overcome this test. You're here now right? You are a fighter. You are strong because you are me."

"But Momma, she is evil like I never saw before! How could this be? Why would God do such a thing to me momma? WHY?! WHY ME?!"

Karen could hear Crush talking out loud as she laid on the couch in an anesthesia trance. Karen was taking notes, scribbling down fast on her note pad, amazed that she can witness such an event with one of the most studied patient subjects known to the medical field on neurology. She wanted to interject, but she knew crush had to go further so she sat there and continued to take notes.

"Crush we don't have time. She's coming. I need you to confront her, and kill her! You will have to challenge yourself in ways you can't imagine."

"What do you mean kill her momma? I'm confused...what do you mean momma?"

Crush looked at her mother with much confusion but before her mother could answer......

"Yeah Momma. What the fuck do you mean! Kill me? Now Momma, you of all mother fuckers should know I can't be killed. You silly bitches. Killing's for kids! You didn't think it would be this easy

momma would ya? Now let's all just have a big old family group hug before I kill the both of you."

"ONYX!" Crush screamed out loud in her direction.

Crush quickly pushed her mother behind her to protect her from Onyx. The three of them stood silently in the kitchen for a few seconds. Onyx quickly lunged out at her grabbing her by the throat once again, lifting her off the floor with Crush's feet 5 inches off the floor. Crush gasped for air while her mother screamed at Onyx to put Crush down. Onyx gritted her teeth, looked at her mother while Crush kicked her feet struggling to get her grip lose. With one hand on Crush's throat, the other hand swung around slapping the mother clear across the kitchen dining room table with force.

Karen quickly saw Crush's body go from calm and relaxed, to screaming and fighting herself? Karen was confused on what was going on, she dropped the pad and pen on the floor and began to count backwards from 5 to 1. She counted repeatedly. It was not working. Crush was fighting for air, as she continued to throw punches at nothing screaming.

"This isn't going to hurt a bit Crush but I need you to stop fighting back now you little bitch. I need my body back, so stop fucking fighting. Why don't you just die already so I can take over what's mines!"

"I will never......let (gasp).....you....(gasp)....take me.....you...you....fucking crazy.......(gasp)....bitch!" While Onyx and Crush were exchanging words in battle, Audrey the mother was creeping up behind Onyx, and stabbed a large butcher knife into Onyx's rib cage. Onyx laughed and looked back at Audrey, not even a bit affected by the large knife fully lunged in her body. Onyx smacked Audrey once again in the opposite direction from the kitchen table, this time sending her flying into the fridge tumbling onto the floor, sliding to the far wall and knocking her out. Crush felt a surge from within herself that she never felt before. Crush, for some reason easily freed herself from Onyx's grip, placing her feet back on the floor, and punched Onyx clear across the room with her landing her right beside their mother. Onyx was surprised for sure but she smiled back at Crush while she wiped the Blood from her lip.

Karen was now shaking Crush hard as hell to wake her up, screaming at the top of her lungs, and out of nowhere, she noticed blood coming from Crush's mouth? She thought she might be biting her lip in the midst of trying to come to. Karen let Crush go to get some tissue as she repeatedly screamed out loud....."Oh my God.....Oh my God!"..Karen was in a frenzy hoping she didn't kill this poor woman.

"So...I see you learned a few new tricks huh...well I have a few tricks of my own fuck -ward. But first, let me get rid of this bitch of a mother that made you! Then I have to get out of here, and let you take my bed in the golden cage of joy you call the lonely room."

"You fucking touch her again and I will put in that lonely room and burn you alive in it every day. If you never saw hell, you sure will see and feel it then. So now I have to end this little visit bitch!." Crush closed her eyes and chanted... "Back to your room.....this is over." Crush opened her eyes.

"Oooops...didn't work this time cunt breath. Didn't I tell you I have a new trick that will finally free me out this fucked up world! Just have to take care of this one to be complete. Don't want her coming back in my fucking head crying about....whyyyy....whyyyy...why did you kill crush...yea, whatever. So say goodbye to your whore mother Crush or you can try to come over here and save her yourself? The choice is yours bitch!"

Onyx grabbed Audrey buy her pony tail dragging her by her head across the floor closer to her. Onyx put Audrey's head in a head lock that she could snap it like a twig in a split second. Crush screamed at the top of her lungs..."NOOOOO!" ran over towards them both on the floor and with her eyes barely open, Audrey whispered low, reaching in Crush's direction... "No......don't let her...touch you Crush" but it was too late, Onyx grabbed Crush's arm and said.

"Are you ready Crush?....Now I COMMAND YOU TO THE LONELY ROOM NOWWW!"

Dr. Karen started to poor cold water on Crush's face from the vase. She tried everything to snap her back. She became so frantic and panic, she screamed out "FUCK THIS SHIT!", and slapped the shit out of Crush..."COME ON YOU BITCH!...DON'T YOU DO THIS TO ME.....COME BACK I SAID! COME ON CRUSH!"...Karen slapped Crush's shivering and shaking body, while her eyes rolled back and forth in her skull. The scene was so loud and intense, that Dr. Thomas Thorp, who happened to have stayed late that night and was getting off the elevator, heard the commotion and came running in her office.

"WHAT THE HELL IS GOING ON KAREN?"

"I DON'T HAVE TIME TO EXPLAIN.....just help me please!"

While she was kneeling over Crush's shivering body, without notice, she went to slap Crush again. With quick speed, Crush's hand caught Karen's wrist. She looked up at Karen with a dark and sinister smile, and with a whole different deeper toned voice, she said to Karen......

"If you slap me again BITCH, I will make sure I make you suffer when I fully take over this body...I know what you look like now bitch and I WILL be back...."

Onyx was surly in control for those few minutes. Back in the world she once caused more chaos than Satan himself. Crush was not the landlord of this property she called her Body! She tossed Karen off the

couch like a rag doll being thrown around the room by a spoiled little brat.

Struggling to get up from the couch, Onyx found it strange to move in the flesh again. She was not use to being out of the Psyche, the lonely room, the brain she was trapped in for several years figuring out how to escape the shell Dr. Kenneth Korvach had trapped her in. She shook standing up to catch her balance.....but suddenly the shaky beautifully shaped body plopped back down on the couch, limp and lifeless. As if she fell fast back to sleep.

Both Doctors Karen and Thomas were frozen stiff. Their eyes and mouths wide open staring at Crush in awe, they could do nothing as they both turned to each other wordless.

Seconds after, Crush leaped up sitting upward facing them both catching her breath, blinking her eyes rapidly. All Crush could say was....

"HOLY FUCKING SHIT!"

CHAPTER NINE:

"The Secret Lair"

The sound of keys rattled as Asteria opened the door to the secret safe house located in Wytkloff, New Jersey. She was greeted by their trained attack Rottweiler named Phoenix, licking Asteria's hand as she patted her head. To call it a safe house was an understatement. This was truly A HOUSE! It was a half a mile drive up the path to get to the high tech security key padded gates that was connected to twenty foot high, brick walls that completely surrounded the entire landscape property of 16 acres of beautiful green scenery. Driving another 1200 yards into the center of the wrap around driveway, two, fifteen foot white marble statues of the great Goddesses Leto and Asteria holding pitchers were located in a manmade marble pond, and had water pouring out of the pitchers back down into the beautiful clear waters. (In Greek mythology, Coeus (also Koios) was the Titan of Intelligence. Titans are the giant sons and daughters of Uranus (Heaven) and Gaia (Earth). With his sister

Phoebe, Titan of Brilliance and the Moon, Coeus fathered Leto and Asteria. Leto copulated with Zeus (the son of fellow Titans Cronus and Rhea) and bore Artemis and Apollo. As with the other Titans, Coeus was overthrown by Zeus and other Olympians). Large Koi fish were swimming in a slow circular motion in the water, with big green lily pads floating on the surface. Asteria had her other hand pressed against her shoulder, applying pressure to stop the bleeding as much as she could on the journey back to the safe house. She continued to kneel down and let Phoenix lick her face as if she was giving her doggie love and affection that only a master should. Leto was outside at the trunk of their car getting the rest of what ammunition was left from the crazy shoot-out with the Chinese. Leto shouted out in Asteria's direction. "You know I'm fucking pissed off that we left our Luis Vutton luggage! Them shits were my favorite fucking traveling bags!" as Leto continued to mumble under her breathe putting the guns in another Gucci bag. Walking up the steps, Phoenix ran out to Leto as well, also jumping up and down following Leto up the steps barking and running in circles. Although Phoenix was acting all shy and childish in her puppy motion, she was a big ass power house of a dog. Phoenix's dog collar was made of black thick leather with Onyx stones placed around the collar.

Leto and Phoenix made their way inside the two 12 foot high oak wood doors that were custom made with metal plates inplanted inside them, making them bullet proof and very hard to break down or to shoot through. Closing the doors, Leto sighed as if her life was dull and boring. The interior design of their house was very pleasing to the eye. In the still of quietness, if one was to yell, the echo would ring aloud throughout the lower level. Black and white marbled chess tiles covered the floors. To the left of the house entrance, was the huge library room with a fire place custom made of marble. Victorian leather couches faced opposite of each other with no end tables at the sides. The couches rested on a huge Persian rug covering the floor's true beauty of the tiles. Each wall had shelves of endless old books and encyclopedias that seem to never end. All the windows had thick burgundy Velvet curtains draping down to the floors, resembling something out of a sexy vampire movie. In addition, there were tall candle holders that stood in the far corners of the room. The thick melted candle wax stuck to the fancy holders as if they have been burning candles for many years over and over each large candle placed in the holders.

To the right of the entrance sat a large room with a white grand piano in the middle of the floor on top of a large Persian area rug. The room had a huge glass wall unit filled with endless DVD movies and a 70 inch flat screen HDTV mounted in the center of the wall. On one wall to the back of the room, it was covered with all types of Rembrandt paintings. These were not copies either, the real deal. Pressed against the same wall was a long custom made cranberry Victorian leather couch, soft and plush. An old large wooden pirate's chest sat beside the Piano, filled with sheet music from Mozart, and many other great composers. One of them was truly a great piano player for sure. Straight passed the back of the entrance, you pass a half moon shaped staircase that lead up to the top level floor. On the right, was the kitchen area through the double French doors. The kitchen and dining room was designed for the Elite life style they lived. But don't be fooled, their kitchen was rigged with all kinds of secret hidden compartments with weapons similar to the movie "The Smiths" in which Angelina Jolie and Brad Pitt had their famous spousal shoot out after they found out they both were spies. The kitchen was loaded with titanium ovens, refrigerators, and stainless steel utensils to brighten up the area.

Quietly walking up the oak wood steps with a cranberry plush Persian carpet softening ever step, Leto carried the bags, as Asteria lead and Phoenix walked by their side. The banister was so thick; you couldn't wrap your hand around it to get a grip. Reaching the top floor, there were two separate wings that had long hallways leading down to their single rooms that met at each corner. No other rooms, just long walls leading down the corridors, also covered with Rembrandt paintings. Leto headed to the left, while Asteria headed to the right. Phoenix was confused on which master to follow. So she let out a soft puff of breath through her nostrils and just laid down on the carpet and got snuggled up against the thick banister overlooking the front entrance. Making her way to her door, Asteria opened it with her good arm. She walked over to her king sized canopy bed and plopped herself on it sighing a sign of relief to be back in her quiet zone. She looked around and realized that they haven't been there in a while, and saw her room needed a serious dusting and touch up. She looked at her shoulder and sighed again, but this time she had a look of tiredness. Not tiredness of the battle, but tiredness of living this lifestyle. She laid back on the bed not worrying about the blood slowly oozing on her quilt set. She looked up at the white soft see through silk cover that draped from the canopy ring over her head. She whispered out loud to herself closing her eyes slowly, "why can't I just get some dick, and call it a life?"

She tried to lift her arm to place it over her face, when the pain shot straight to her chest making her scream real loud. She rolled her eyes and shouted "FUCK!" and jolted back up, sitting still gritting her teeth. Leto came to her door slowly, looking in on her sister with concern. Normally she would make a wise joke, but with the sisterly instincts, she felt something was defiantly different in her sister's face. Leto walked over to her sister placing her hand over her good shoulder softly.

"Let's take a look at that shoulder Asteria?"
"Yeah, just go in my bathroom and get the fix shit quick kit."
"Ok, I'm on it"

Before going to make her way to the bathroom, Leto brushed the loose hairs from Asteria's face, giving her a smile as she walked away. Asteria sat there and started to think to herself, who the fuck could have betrayed them? Who tried to send them to their deaths? Who was in with the Chinese? Although it could only have been the one who gave them the mission, Asteria knows that everything is not always what it appears to be in this game. Leto returned with the first aid kit. Asteria was now back to her fearless self as she pulled her shirt completely off with both arms, showing no pain. She grabbed the hot cloth from Leto and began to wipe the wounded area with it. She snatched the bottle of alcohol out of Leto's hand, opened the top, and poured enough to sterilize the gunshot wound. Leto opened the first aid kit passing her the large tweezers and a wooden stick to bite down on while digging for the new bronze colored jewelry that was lodged in her flesh. Asteria didn't take the wooden stick to bite down on, as she dug the tweezers in her shoulder trying to locate the bullet. She gritted her teeth even harder as she continued to dig and search. Leto never saw her sister act so aggressive towards a situation like this. She just stood there wiping the blood that spilled down Asteria shoulder, avoiding it from going onto her bra or between her breast. Asteria gritted.

"Almost got it....almost...got it!"

As she pulled the bullet out, she let out a loud shout, "FUCKING MOTHER FUCKERS!"

Asteria placed the bullet in her hand and just stared at it.
"Oh.....it's on mother fuckers!"
Leto finally did what she does.
"That's what the fuck I'm talking about!" Laughing real loud again with the Muah-hahaha evil laugh.

Asteria got up and told Leto to turn on the computer while she took a shower to clean up and patch the wound. Leto asked if she was hungry? Asteria replied, "Only for revenge" as she continued to strip and make her way to the bathroom. Leto, young and full of energy, insisted that she eat something and drink water before she dehydrates and passes out from lack of substances. Crazy, but much educated. They both were. All they were taught was to read, read, and read some more. The key to knowing, is to know what the fuck you need to know by learning all there is to know, by reading and researching. While Leto made her way down to the kitchen, Asteria's walked into her bathroom. Her body movements were sensed by the motion detectors, the hot water in her walk-in shower with no glass doors or shower curtains, came flowing down. The bathroom was custom made like everything else in their modern home. The stainless steel shower head came straight out the ceiling. In the center of the bathroom floor were tiled steps that lead down to an open area with a drain. It was the size of a bath house room. She had all the perks to go with the room and so much space that her vanity area had an all white plush cotton love seat that faced a large mirror that covered the entire wall. Her bathroom was all white tiled with a large porcelain sink and toilet. She loved her open space. The bathroom was so big that the mirror wouldn't even fog up from the heat.

She let the hot water run down her bare body as every drop graced her perfect shape. Standing there looking like a young Playboy Bunny centerfold model, sexy and all, the blood from her shoulder ran down the drain in a circular motion. Playing with her belly piercing, she began to suds herself up with that good smelling foam soap from Bath & Body Works. These girls were so perfect in every definition. Pure perfection. After a short session of washing, Asteria's eyes popped open with sureness that she knew who set them up. She quickly walked up the steps to the towel rack, dried herself off, grabbed the gauze pads and white surgical tape and sat down on the couch to patch up the wound. She mumbled to herself aloud "It has to be him?" She shook her head back and forth in deep thought wondering if this was the truth. She patched up the wound, wrapped herself in her bathrobe and exited the bathroom. She headed fast towards her oak wood desk that had three large monitor screens to the computer. Asteria sat down and began to type on the keypad.

Meanwhile, after putting all the bags and guns away, and changing into something more comfortable, Leto made her way down in the kitchen to make a few ham and cheese sandwiches with hot bowls of tomato soup on the side. Phoenix was still asleep in the same spot by the staircase. Even though the two sisters were single with no men in their lives, they both wore sexy sleep wear. Leto put on a pink laced ruffled teddy with fuzzy bunny slippers on her feet and walked down the steps sliding the palm of her hand down the smooth banister. Making a right, heading towards the kitchen, on a small antique wooden table placed against the wall, she grabbed a small remote that would allow her to utilize the music system in the kitchen. Entering the kitchen she pressed the track selection on the system and the intro to Faith Evans CD began to play aloud.

Leto began to sing along with Faith Evans to the song "Soon As I Get Home". The song echoed through the house. Leto might not be a

Faith Evans, but if she had the chance to make a career change to singing, she just might be signed just as fast as she could pull a trigger. The girl could blow a note. She opened the refrigerator door and took out the ingredients she needed to make the menu at hand. Placing them on the black and white swirled pattern marble counter, she began to sing louder.

"Soon as I get home, I'll make it up to you....babay, I do what I gotta dooo.....This my shit yo!" she said with a big smile on her face as she bopped her head and swayed her hips from side to side in a slow grind motion. Placing a knife in her other hand twirling it around on a fast motion, then stopping it with a fast grip, she dipped the knife in the mayo jar and began to spread it on the bread. While doing so, she began to fantasize about having a young boy, around her age, placing his hands on her hips pressing his hard erect cock against the crease of her ass while she continued to make the sandwiches. Her mind continued to get more graphic as she reached for the cheese and ham to make the meal complete. She imagined as she leaned over the counter top, him placing his hands lower on her thighs making his way up and closer to her coochie area. Even so deep in her fantasy, she still mumbled out loud "Oh baby yes." Still swaying to the sound of the music, she began to close her eyes in a pause and grind her upper pelvic area up against the counter, as if his force pushed her body to do so. She can feel his muscular defined body all on her back as he pushed his finger into her cooch slowly. Although there was no real man there, her pussy began to get wet. Now she was completely standing there in a still position frozen in her fantasy with her eyes closed, moaning to herself, he turned her around and lifted her up by both her thighs with strength and sat her on the counter with her legs spread and wrapped around his waist. He kissed her softly all up and down her neck with passionate movements. She placed both her hands down the small of his back making her way in the trousers she imagined him wearing. She gripped both his ass cheeks pulling him and his cock closer to her. He pushed her back just enough so he could pull his dick out and move her panties to the side to slide up inside her. Standing there, her body jerked as if it was actually happening. Then in the heat of him entering her wet and hot pussy, she leaned back to push all the contents on the counter onto the floor so they could get a better fuck on the counter. His cock was so huge and thick, she can feel every inch of it while he pumped her ever so tender body. It seemed as if every pump went along with the lyrics that came out the speaker. Faster and faster they both gripped each other's hips, him to pull himself deeper, and her, pushing because the force was too painful but yet enjoyable at the same time. Leto was a pain freak. She enjoyed pain. She wanted pain. As she imagined them coming closer and closer to climax, she grabbed herself down below with her free hand rubbing her pussy to get an even better feel to climax. By this time she was ready. Ready to explode. Ready to cum. "I'm Ready......I'm ready.....oh baby.....I'm ready!" she screamed out loud.

"Ready for what?" Asteria said entering the kitchen.

Leto paused and opened her eyes wide with a frustrated look on her face.

"ARE YOU FUCKING SERIOUS YO?".......SERIOUSLY?"

"Leto you are a fucking freak. Was it that good?"

"Yes it was."

"You would think with all this shit we do, we could at least get some dick along the way. I understand."

"No you don't."

"Yes....I do."

NO NIGGA....you don't!"

Asteria looked at Leto and began to laugh out loud. They both began to laugh together.

"I hope you wash your hands before you finish making those sandwiches." Asteria said still giggling.

"I should use my cum as the Mayo, and put that shit right on your bread for that shit."

"Now that's some nasty shit. Although I wouldn't mind some woman cumming in my mouth right about now."

"I hear that hot shit sis."

Leto and Asteria continued to have idle chat about their secret fantasies and desires while making the sandwiches that should have been served an hour ago. The music continued to play in the background.

Sade was the next CD in the deck to give that smooth soulistic vibe to the atmosphere. The two beautiful, sexy and very dangerous sisters sat as if they did not have a care in the world and enjoyed their meal. Moments later they found their way back to their rooms after exchanging kisses and hugs as only the closest of kin will do. Leto went fast to sleep in her plush bed. Asteria had work to do for sure. She was not one bit tired after all that happened in their murderous missions.

Sitting back at her desk, she tapped on her keypad opening files and scrolling through documents that might have the info she believed could give her the answer to her question. Who could have given the Chinese the heads up about their mission and the order to wipe them out? After two hours of pure patience going through file after file, reviewing missions from the past to the present, she paused for a second and went back to a closed file and realized that there was one name that stood out in that document. Why was this person's name even mentioned in this file? She thought to herself out loud, "What the fuck does he have to do with this mission?" She tapped her finger nail against her teeth and began to put the pieces together. She leaned back in her leather seat and began to sway back and forth in deep thought. Was she sure? Going over many scenarios in her head she was certain it was him. Her eyes squinted and as her teeth gritted with anger, Asteria pushed her neck from left to right cracking the bones making a loud sound as if she was preparing to have a hell of a fight. That was certainly the case. She jumped out her seat and walked straight to her closet and pulled out her go kill a mother fucker outfit. Black leather tight pants, black tank top, black leather motorcycle jacket that hugged her body tight, black leather calf length boots with a 4 inch heal, looking sexy to kill was the motto. Pressing a secret lever button on the side of the picture near her closet, a secret wall flipped from one side to the other displaying massive weapons of destruction. Thirty hand guns of all assorted flavors from the M1911 to a simple 9 MM, twenty automatic assault rifles MPSKs, HK21, a few M16s, AK47s, the newest hand grenades, land mines, fifteen shot guns of all different designs including three Spas 12s. Almost every weapon you can use on one of those Xbox games, or seen in a real old Arnold or Bruce Willis movie. Knives hung from ceiling to floor in each corner of the room. Out of all the weapons, she only grabbed one nickel plated commando hand gun fully loaded with two extra clips.

Trying not to wake Leto, Asteria made her way down to the garage were their collection of motor toys were located, two Lambroginis, an Aston Martin, two GMC Black tinted trucks, a Hummer, and a Bentley two door coupe. But Asteria was a rider. Her babies were the three Ducatis, one red, one black and one silver. In the still of the night, Asteria road out into the dark on the black one with a mission. The quiet sound of her engine faded down the path as the thrust of her speed tossed leaves around behind her in a whirlpool formation. Just as she thought she was not being watched, and no one could possibly know their secret safe house, two men wearing all black and their faces covered with tight ski mask with night vision goggles carrying a matching pair of L96A1s with infrared scopes stood up from behind a bush on the far left side of the house looking up at what entry point window could be used. Leto still comfortable in her sleep, had no clue as to what was about to happen. Maybe their reputations for being the youngest and hardest targets to kill will be justified. Silently one signaled the other with a hand gesture for him to go in one direction while he went in another. The loud sounds of crickets rubbing the legs together filled the still night around the house. The moonlight was bright enough to give a light shade to every corner turned to the house. One of the men was making his way around a corner looking from left to right, when he should have been looking up. Leto was hanging upside down on a black rope entwined in her thighs still in her sexy panties and top, she whispered in his right ear as he turned once more to the left. "Hey handsome" The man didn't even respond or act surprised as he sighed softly through his black mask. He knew his death would be quite and quick. He stood still for a few seconds and realized nothing happened. He turned his head as slow as he could just to see Leto was not hanging there anymore. He frantically looked up, left, and right repeatedly as he backed up away from the wall slowly. Like a ninja in the mist, she was there and then she was gone. He started to realize that whatever training he had gone through to become a hit man, was truly under minded by that move she just did. It seemed as every sound and movement from every direction, the Owl in the tree, the shadows of swaying branches from the wind, the leaves rolling around on the lawn, and even his own heartbeat, gave him a chill that it might be her making her way to attack again. Even with night vision on his side, how did she creep up on him? They forgot one thing that wasn't written in the assassin's manual booklet in his back pocket. This was their territory and they stood less of a chance of surviving than a slug crawling itself into a big bowl of salt.

He still knew his mission had to continue, so on he went still playing the Black Ops movements hunched over pointing his gun ahead and making his way around the next corner. Being more cautious this time, he looked up and down. He went to step around the corner slowly when under his foot was a large object that stopped him short. He thought to himself, if I take my eyes off the direction I should be looking in, it could be my death. So he looked down real quick and then popped his head back up. He couldn't help but to look back down. He thought his eyes were deceiving him when in fact they were correct. It was his partner's arm severed from his body, still with the hand gripping the gun. He continued to walk very slow following the trail to his partner's other severed arm a few more feet away from the other. He took a few more steps towards the front lawn in the dark and heard a small thud sound hit the lawn. The severed head of his partner hit the grass from being thrown from above. As he looked in fear his hand began to shake just a little when she whispered again closely behind him, "I didn't forget you sexy." Before he could turn around to let off a shot, he himself was shot in the neck. He thought he was done, for sure. Reaching for the area on the left side of his neck that he thought would be a gushing hole of blood, was just a feather attached to a tranquilizing sleeping dart. A few seconds before falling into a coma like sleep, the man saw Leto standing right before him in her sexy night wear with a sinister smile, and just enough energy to hear her words as he faded out, "Your gonna wish I killed you. Because, now I have to question you. Muah-Hahaha............."

CHAPTER TEN:

"Down The Rabbit Hole We Go"

After they both read the document files, Candice and Michelle had to figure out their next move, and it just got more complicated. Michelle could not believe her eyes still after reading all the names that were documented. Candice and Michelle talked about what they should do first, and what avenues to take before going over to Crush's house to question her about the pictures with her and Black Butterfly. A few hours passed by as they both got enough rest for the next morning. 9:45 am displayed on the clock as Michelle wiped her sleepy eyes and yawned. Before she could get her tired ass up, the knocking on her Hotel room door somehow annoyed her. Candice was still hard asleep on the bed next to her. Michelle made her way to the door, looking through the peep hole seeing Antonio peeping back with a big smile on his face. She opened the door still in her night wear. Antonio entered the room and couldn't help reacting to the beautifully shaped Agent.

"Nice mami, ju are so beautiful in the morning. I think I might have to reconsider my initial reason for waking ju up?"

"You have got to be kidding" ....As she yawned again and smiled at him. "Listen papi chulo, you're not ready for this southern humming bird"

As Candice woke up laughing at the conversation, she also was dressed in her night wear as she let the sheet fall down from the top part of her perfect tender breast. Antonio then shifted his eyes in her direction and commented again in his latin sexy tone.

"Neber mind about the one, when I can have dos." He began to rub his palms together in a soft motion. A second passed before Antonio was slapped so hard on his ass by Agent Mee Sun Young, it made him jump.

"That's right Spanish fly, that ass belongs to me." Mimi said as she walked in the room. Michelle and Candice began to chuckle at Antonio because his face turned beet red. Antonio smiled and plopped himself on the bed where Candice was sitting up wrapping her loose hair up in a bun. The white T-shirt she had on with the Nike swoosh symbol, did nothing for hiding her erect nipples. Antonio couldn't help but to notice them as he tried to shift his eyes away. A moment of silence filled the air, because everyone noticed him staring at first. Michelle was the first to jump in the luxurious Hotel shower to wash up and get dressed before they started their day in the Big Apple. Candice was getting her outfit ready and talking with Mimi about her being debriefed on the Crush Onyx case. Time passed with lots of talk about Crush and the crazy mental defect she was born with. While putting on her jacket, Michelle gave Candice a silent stare about the documents left on the night table. She nudged her head to the left telling her to take that info off the table before Antonio or Mimi started to ask questions about them. Candice picked up the folder and put it in her briefcase without being noticed. While standing in the Hotel hallway waiting for the elevator, Candice's phone rang. It was Allgood on the other end.

"Hello sir."

"Hello Candice. Did you get a good night sleep? I hope so. Today is going to be a long day for you and Michelle. First, because this mission is off the record and not being documented, you girls have to plant cameras and tap her phones with equipment from an outside connection. I have an old retired CIA friend off the grid that owes me a few favors. He has everything you ladies need to make this happen. He is expecting your visit. After he retired, he opened up little cigar shop on 36th Street between 7th and 8th Avenues on the Westside of Manhattan. He still does some work on and off for the Government from time to time. Let's just say, his special talent doesn't go recorded because of its nature. So if you find yourselves in a situation that requires heavy fire power, he has all you need. I will continue to cover you both from this end. I have you both on personal time off. You have all the time you need. And remember, if the shit gets real thick, you ladies are on your own. I'm also using a scrambled coded phone line that can't be traced. He also has two phones for the both of you so no one can pick up any signals in the air waves. Make sure you brief Michelle on all that I told you. The numbers only connect to these specific phones. Be careful, and call only when necessary."

"Yes sir, will do."

Candice hung up the phone and made up some bullshit undercover mission story on the ride down in the elevator to Mimi and Antonio. The first thing they needed to do, was shop for a new look and get out of those white collar F.B.I. dress code clothes. As they made their way on the city streets exiting the Hotel, Candice told Mimi what they planned on doing for most of the day. Shop! Mimi laughed and pointed them in the direction they should be heading in, 34th Street, which happen to be near where their connect was located for the equipment they needed to plant in Crush's apartment. Mimi suggested not to drive being that it was a short, nice walk down 7th Avenue from 46th to 34th Street. Plus they can sight see, and might like to window shop along the way and enjoy what the Big Apple can offer as far as fashion. Michelle and Candice waved goodbye to Antonio and Mimi like young excited teenagers finally being released from their parent's grip to explore the Big City on their own for the first time.

On their way down 7th Avenue, Candice began to brief Michelle on what Allgood told her. Michelle was excited to be on a mission that didn't require all the paper work afterwards. They stopped off at the first Chase Bank they found to withdraw some cash from the secret account. Michelle was the name it was under, so she went all out immediately by making a withdrawal of $5,000. She figured this shit was free and why not take full advantage of it now, because once it was over, it was over. Candice put a smile on her face as well, looking like, fuck that shit, I'm down, $2,500 each, straight down the middle. Just like when they were little girls and one dollar seemed like a hundred. They would split it 50/50. They walked out of the bank like that old school TV show from the 70's, "Lavern and Shirley" holding on to each other, locked arm to arm smiling. They made a few stops here and there at little boutique shops and tried on outfits and shoes as they made funny faces at each outfit saying what was good and what was bad. Michelle was the real diva in a small way. Even though she rarely got out to have a good time from all the work of being an F.B.I. Agent, she knew what style was. They both had very short relationships after joining the force. A little ass here and there, a few one night fucks but they never could get too serious with men. Plus, most men would shy away at the thought of a woman, who can look into whether they have a dark past or are unfaithful. Michelle or Candice would be able to find out about it with a click of a key stroke from the FBI database and could make their ass disappear in a heartbeat and no one would find their ass either. No man wanted to take that chance.

Finally reaching 34th Street, they both stopped dead in their tracks and marveled at the sight of Macy's. One of the most sought out shopping stores for tourist out of state, and the country. They made their way through the swinging doors and could not believe how big this store was.

"DAMN! Do you see this shit Candice?"

"Holy crap Michelle! The first floor is as big as most of our mall areas in a whole!"

"Wow! This is going to be crazy fun."

"Where should we go first?"

Michelle looked at Candice with a big smile on her face. Both of them took a deep breath and said, "SHOES!"

They laughed and asked one of the department store managers what floor was the shoes on. The woman was tall and beautiful. She pointed in the direction of the elevators and told them how many parts of the store had shoes, and it would take at least 5 hours just to see all the shoe collections Macy's had to offer. Michelle leaned on Candice and whispered in her ear "Damn that's a tall bitch". Candice tried not to laugh as the woman also told them about the perfume section and where they could get the latest hand bags and purses, as well. They made their way to the perfume section because it was on the ground level, and they were there anyway. Candice and Michelle were swamped by many workers trying to get them to purchase a bottle of the perfume in their sections. Michelle stepped a few feet away from Candice to look at the displays in the glass counters as Candice took a few sniffs of several scents. Not even a few seconds passed before the first brother attempted to make small chat with her.

"Yo love. What's good ma? Damn girl, that's good money right there. What's really good though? I'm just sayin ma".

Michelle was not use to the New York slang at all.

"What?" she answered with a crazy puzzled look in her eyes.

"I'm sayin what's good wit you ma? You seein' somebody? I'm diggin you like crazy."

"What...?" Again Michelle was confused.

Michelle couldn't help it anymore. She burst out in a loud laugh grabbing her chest like, is this guy serious? She even leaned into him placing her forehead on his shoulder laughing loud as hell drawing attention in their direction. The brother was tall, light skinned and very attractive. But his New York slang was so crazy to her ears.

"Oh! It's like that!" He said with a smile as he backed up just a little. Not displaying embarrassment, but was confused if he was being dissed or she was taken by surprise on his attempt to even approach her.

"No...no...sorry. I'm just not from New York. I'm a southern bird, and we don't talk like that down south. I just don't know what you are saying. I mean, I know you trying to get at me, but some slang I just don't know. But no."

"Ok cool. I will stop with the slang and just introduce myself all over again. Hi. My name is Jamal. May I ask you yours?"

"It's Michelle. Nice to meet you Jamal."

"Nice to meet you for sure...I mean...It's my pleasure to meet you too Michelle. So, what brings you to the Big Apple?"

"I'm here on vacation. Me and my girlfriend are here to enjoy some quality time in the city and have some fun."

"OH SHIT! Your lesbians? That's cool too. Maybe she won't mind putting me in the middle and make a sandwich."

Michelle again grabbed her chest and began to laugh as Candice walked over at the same time.

"I SAID...DAMNNN! She is just as fine as you. White girl too? Look at those eyes. My God sweetie, them eyes are so light blue, we can swim in them, and the blond long hair? DAMNNN! Please let a brother get down for one night?"

Candice looked at Michelle with the same puzzled look in her eyes. Then she smiled and turned back in the direction of Jamal and got a little closer and whispered in his ear.

"You have to make sure you can keep up with me. You know how us white girls are. We like it long and hard for many hours. Can you handle us both?"

Michelle leaned in too.

"Yeah Jay...and I like it deep in my mouth and down my throat. Can you get it all down my throat big daddy?"

Jamal then realized they were playing with him and making him all excited for no reason. He twisted up his lips with a small smile attached and replied back in a chuckle.

"Ah...I see how this is going ladies. It doesn't hurt to try. I was just saying yo. Fuck it though. I tried right."

Michelle answered with a sarcastic laugh.

"Yes you did sexy. Don't get me wrong, you're cute and all, but no, and you didn't even ask what it is that I do for a living?"

"Ok. What do you two do for a living?"

Michelle and Candice opened their jackets and flashed their F.B.I. badges.

"OH HELL NO! Nah, no way! You chicks are the Feds? Ok. It was a pleasure, but not, so I'm going to let you two do what you do, and.....I'm out!"

Jamal backed away real fast and immediately made a u-turn and walked off fast. He almost knocked over a man in passing. Candice shook her head and laughed at the scene. Michelle grabbed Candice by her arm and pulled her close and began to walk down the aisle towards the next section of the store. They spent about three hours shopping and having the best time they ever had. Exiting the store with both arms full of bags, of course the best designers. Gucci, Prada, Louie, Vera Wang and a few Urban brands, Lady Rocawear and Sean John. It was time to head towards the cigar shop to meet the C.I.A. connect, and get the equipment needed to bug Crush's apartment. What a better way to enter the cigar shop, not looking like Feds, but like two wealthy ladies who have a taste for cigars like big time Business men do. It was easy for them to find the cigar shop being it was only two city blocks up to 36th. Entering the cigar shop, they noticed it was kind of empty. The sweet smell of scented cherry cigars filled the air as they made their way to the counter to be greeted by a young slim Indian cashier with long silky hair that went down her back almost reaching her upper thigh area. She had the most beautiful red skin tone a woman could ever want. She was so pure from her race, she never had to want or need a tanning salon in her life. They approached the counter with bags in their arms, and with a smile Michelle said, "Hi sweetie! Can I speak to your manager? He's expecting us."

"May I ask what your names are?" The young woman answered.

"Yes, sure, it's Michelle Blake and Candice Sums."

The young woman looked both ways and asked them to follow her as she lead them to an area that seemed to be a fitting room with a long thick draped curtain. The walls had wooden cabinets with glass doors exposing many selections of different imported cases of cigars. She slid the curtains closed, and asked them to look up at the camera that was in the far left corner of the room.

"Now please stare directly into the lens and please remain as still as possible."

The woman left them alone and closed the curtain on her way out. They both looked as instructed, when an infrared beam of light shot out the camera scanning their eyes. In a few seconds when it was over, the wall in front of them that had all the cabinets, shifted real fast and opened with a soft burst of air, as if it was sealed air tight. Then suddenly, over a small speaker planted in the wall, a voice told them to please follow the steps to the end that lead to a secret lower level under the store property. Doing so, Michelle and Candice found themselves in a large room that looked custom made from wall to wall. It was better than the hotel suite at the Marriott. This room had wall to wall plush carpet, a glass custom made bar that seats about ten people, a very large luxurious Pool table, a movie theater screen hanging in the far back with the movie theater plush entertainment leather couch set to match, and a grand piano in the middle of the floor. It was kind of dim in the room, with one lamp lighting the area where the man was sitting in a large leather chair with the back of the chairs facing them in front of a large custom made glass desk with four computer monitors lit up. They could only see the very top of his head as the smoke from the cigar he was smoking filled the air.

"Come over here ladies". The man said with a scratching old tone in his voice.

He sounded very seductive at the same time. Michelle and Candice walked over towards the man, when he spun the chair around to face them. He was a handsome older man, almost resembling the actor Sean Connery, from the original 007 James Bond movies. He was clean shaved, had full head of grey hair, and wore a pin striped Brooks Brothers suit with a white collar shirt and a silk striped pink tie.

"So, you are the two ladies my friend, Stubs has been raving about. He tells me you are about to cross over from the boring field work y'all gals are use to. Y'all are about to get your cherries popped going off the grid. This Crush Onyx has been a headliner for many years in the business we're in. I must tell you, many have tried to capture her because of the unique nature. But ladies, this is about to get way more complicated then you can ever imagine. Onyx, the alter ego side of Ms. Crush, has built quite a reputation in the underground world. I suggest you kick your shoes off, and have a drink while I give you a brief history of what you think is simple about your situation...Have a seat please."

There was two leather chairs on the other side of his large desk. They made their way around the desk and sat down to continue listening. Michelle did help herself to a glass of spritzer before listening to the rest of what the man had to say. Candice just took her jacket off placing it on the back of her chair and sat as well.

"First, you can call me Mr. 9. The boys in my unit named me that many years ago. I'm sure you can figure out why. Well, one of the missions I survived and lived through to tell happens to be connected to yours truly, Ms. Crush Onyx. Well, Onyx, when she had her reign over the use of the flesh. I was assigned to assassinate someone, they called him Vanish. I remember him just a bit, because we took our training at the same time from the C.I.A. academy back when. He graduated and throughout the years of missions, he somehow lost his grip, and became rouge. They have been trying to catch him since. Little did I know, later to find out, he was recruited by Onyx, and became her team trainer who helped build the Serial Killing Cult known as "THE SANDBOX". Make no mistake ladies; the Black Butterfly was one of her lower level followers. From what I gathered so far, after it became too much for me to handle, I was finding there had to be at least forty strong followers in her camp. Yes, they are everywhere and can be anybody all at once. If she is to resurface, which I believe she will, her most prized possessions are her daughters, Asteria and Leto, the Twin Assassins! Oh yes, I have all the detailed Intel on her. Which brings us to this point. How can we stop her? Too much red tape ladies. This woman is covered from the most highest elite. I mean she has protection from people even in the White House. Someone, or a few are involved in this craziness. Dr. Korvach was a very smart and dangerous man. I believe he is a fucking evil genius, if I might say. That man has done more shit to fuck with people's minds than the government can ever do. Who do you think makes up all these microbiological test serums to test on human subjects? Dr. Korvach has created some new wicked stuff ladies. All his studies lie within that woman's DNA I believe. They secretly tried to duplicate his work for many years after the sudden disappearance of Korvach to figure out how he did it. Hair samples, taking DNA from glasses she drank from. Even someone, somehow got urine and stool samples. God knows how they did that without her knowing. But what I'm trying to say is; I will go as far as I can to helping you ladies out on this. All the equipment is in that duffle bag by the bar. The phones are in those two cases on the bar. If you need Guns and Ammo that's not registered by the government, just come back. If you make it back in one piece."

"Why would you say that Mr. 9? When all we're doing is planting bugs and cameras to monitor Crush and see what else we can find out. Besides, Onyx is inactive forever. Wasn't she destroyed, or locked away in Crush's mind? Never to come back?" Candice asked.

"I don't think you are listening. I said she is already being monitored by her people and the Government as well. As I was already informed, didn't you shortly meet with a British Agent, who I must remind you was murdered here at the Airport, in plain day light. Open your eyes ladies. How do you think that happened? You are being watched for some reason and must play a part in this puzzle somehow. If not, then there would have been three body bags leaving the Airport. All I can say is, something is about to happen real big. Too much old stuff is resurfacing at a fast pace. Maybe you should ask Mimi about her past as well. The Chinese Triads head killed in Manhattan at a secret family meeting? The Agent dead at the Airport? Miss Crush had an episode at the Hospital as well. I told Stubs, you ladies are either crazy, or have the ambition of a slug trying to make it across a speeding traffic highway. Either way, Good Luck and like I said in other words, watch your backs. Everyone is a suspect, even the FBI. Don't be blind ladies. Keep your eyes open and don't fall asleep for a second. It can cost you your lives. I believe someone wants you two alive or we wouldn't be having this conversation."

Michelle crossed her legs and began to give Mr. 9 a look like she wasn't too happy about the information he was giving to them. She also turned to Candice and grunted under her breath, waiting for Candice to respond.

"Well, that was most informative Mr. 9. Bravo. I appreciate all the briefing on this matter but that's not enough! You say that's about as far as you are willing to go. Well, I need more! Much more! In fact, I need all the shit you have, names, locations, anything that might help us survive. As you put it, to shut this whole thing down, it might have gotten thick for you, but I'm just getting fucking started! This bitch and her stupid silly Cult is going down! One by one if necessary! The Sandbox? What kind of silly ass shit is that? Well, I'm about to apply so much heat, they all will be turned into wine glasses added to my collection by the time we are done! So you can save all the bullshit scare tactic shit, and start giving me the next mother fucker we need to go get! I found Black Butterfly, and that was the easy way out for her ass. So you see Mr. 9, 10, 11, whatever silly ass names you people give each other. I don't have time for this bullshit! So show me what you got, or we can dossie doe right here, right now! Cause we ain't leaving 'till you give us more than that!"

Michelle turned her chair back in the direction of Mr.9. This time she had that ghetto black girl smirk on her face. She began to tap the heel of her shoe on her ankle waiting for his response. Mr. 9 leaned back in his chair with both arms folded over one another and took a deep breath and began to laugh as he spun himself around exposing the back of the chair in their direction again.

"Stubs told me you two were his babies. Now I see why. You think you have it all covered but I will give you one lead name, and that one lead will be the one that starts a chain of events that will take you both on a journey that will alter your lives forever. You think it was thick for me? It's about to get even thicker for you. BRIAN CENTURY! Find him, and that's where you begin."

He must have already anticipated their reaction and handed them a USB stick with all the information on Brian Century. The stick contained all his history from childhood to present, pictures of his family, mother, father, sisters and one brother; addresses, work history, dental records and all.

"Now please take a box of Cubans on your way out. That's on me. You're gonna need a good Cigar to celebrate if you live, ladies."

Candice and Michelle stood up out their seats, as Michelle took the USB stick and put it in her pocket. Candice replied that they will be back if it gets too thick, and smiled at Mr.9 as they made their way back up the stairs to exit.

Returning back to the hotel, Michelle and Candice dropped the bags on the beds and began to discuss their strategy on planting the bugs and cameras in Crush's condo and what to do about questioning Brian Century. First, they gathered all the surveillance equipment together and went through scenarios discussing their plan of action if the mission was ever compromised and Crush was to walk in on them planting the bugs and cameras. Michelle sat down at the desk and turned her laptop on to look at the info on Brian.

Candice was trying to figure out how the damn equipment worked, and laughed out loud. "You know Michelle, I wish we had training on this shit?"

"Let's just hope we don't fuck this up."

"Do you think this is over our head? I mean really...I'm starting to feel it's not worth it anymore. I been chasing a Phantom, in some sort of a way, but we know who it is. Does that make sense Michelle?"

"Oh girl please. If it wasn't for Onyx, we would be chasing terrorist and getting shot at all damn day or pushing paper work in the lower level of Langley Head Quarters. Remember, we worked our butts off to get where we are today in this field. So stop thinking crazy and it's because of you being so dedicated, we broke the glass ceiling."

"Thank you Michelle. I can always depend on you making light of everything. But c'mon, you have to admit, this shit is getting real thick."

"I'm kind of getting a little wet thinking of this mission. I mean. What the hell was all this for then, the training, the Academy. My father died for this ya know, making a difference in this world, keeping the crazies off the streets. I refuse to let him die in vain."

Candice paused before answering Michelle. She knew Michelle's father's death was hard on her and Michelle had this void to fill because of the nature of her father's death. The criminal was never caught and still at large. Michelle felt that if she could catch as many criminals as she can, it would somehow fill the void of her father's murder.

"I know Michelle. Yeah, you're right. I'm getting all soft and what not. What you got over there?"

"Well, it looks like we have to take a little trip to Iowa State to find this Brian guy. His parents are separated. He has his own house, so that makes it easier to cut through questioning his parents. Remember Dr. Korvach's document files on him? We know he has been experimented on, so no telling what he will remember, if anything at all. He was under some sort of spell. Maybe he won't be able to give us anything to work with?"

"Well I don't care about that at this point. He's connected. And we will break him if we have too. He's Crush's boyfriend and Mr. 9 wouldn't give us this information if there wasn't more to it with him."

"You got that right. So let's gear up and head to Crush's house and hope she's out and about."

"Let's Ride........"

CHAPTER ELEVEN

"The Brian Century Flashback"

Brian was born in Henry County, located in the beautiful Southern Drift Plain of Southeast Iowa. The population ratio for African Americans was very small, 94.78% white, 1.49% black. Brian was a biracial baby. His mother was white and father was black. He went to the local schools in his County, Salem Elementary, and then Mt. Pleasant High School. His education was good considering he attended predominately white schools. His father was a Lawyer, and his mother was a teacher. Brian had all the perks of both worlds. In his earlier teens Brian suffered from a case of depression because he felt out of place being a product of a biracial relationship. Growing up in his county, he suffered more from racial jokes from students and local bullies in his town. Even though he was born with a silver spoon in his mouth, his battle trying to defend his mixed bloodline lead him to become an addict of pain killers he started using after and during his basketball games. Brian's depression fits slowed down more and more after his first championship high school game, in which he lead his team to victory. But his parents felt he still needed some private therapy for his condition. They heard so much about Dr. Korvach and how he was at the top of his studies for mental illnesses. They wanted their son to have the best, so they paid for the best.

In 1987, a couple of months after being treated at the Kenneth Korvach Estate, and after graduating High School, Brian fell in love with the most beautiful girl he had ever seen after a group session one hot summer day. He couldn't believe his eyes. Not only was she beautiful, but she was Black and in Iowa, the odds of that happening was slim to none. For the first few weeks, Brian pretended to be depressed just so he could stay at the Estate and somehow get the guts to introduce himself to Crush. Finally one day in the library of the Estate, Brian found himself sitting at the same table as Crush. Actually, he was sitting there first reading a Superman comic book, when Crush came from nowhere and sat down a couple chairs down from him. She had a thick novel in her hand. She placed the book on the table as she pulled her hair up in a pony tail and wrapped a scrunchy around it and put it up in a bun. She glanced over and noticed him staring from the corner of his eye. She smiled and let out a chuckle as if she didn't notice him staring.

Brian cleared his throat and put the comic book down slowly and grabbed the law book he was originally suppose to be reading. He didn't want his first impression to be a bad one. He wanted to look educated, not like a little boy who still reads comic books. They pretended not to want to break the silence until...

"What issue is that you're reading?" Crush whispered across the table.

"What?" He answered with his voice cracking.

"I said...what issue of Superman are you reading?"

Brian's face began to flush and turn red as he squirmed in his seat and tried to remain cool in his posture.

"Its #96"

"Cool. I have numbers 7-75"

"WHAT!" Brian's voice echoed through the library making a few heads turn in their direction wondering what was going on over at their table to make him say that so loud. Crush put her face in her shirt and tried to stop herself from laughing even louder. Brian began to do the same. Crush looked around and decided to just get up and go over to a seat closer to him. She sat down right beside him. The smell of her perfume made Brian fall into a short state of stillness. Crush looked at his reaction and commented…"You like what I'm wearing?"

"Umm...Yes--umm...yeah"

"Why did you say it like that?...oh, first...hi, my name is Crush."

"Umm...Hi, my name is Brian."

"So why did you?"

"Are you serious? You have issues 7-75? Do you know the value of those issues Crush?"

"Actually...yes. My father was a collector. There are only 27 existing copies of Issue 7 in the whole world. The value will go up in the years to come."

"I know. I'm surprised that a...a...you know...A girl collects comics."

"And what's wrong with that Brian?"

They both paused and caught themselves staring into each other's eyes for a few seconds. The mood completely shifted and filled the area with a small hint of lust. They quickly shifted their eyes away from each other and pretended that the moment wasn't happening. They both felt the energy in the air. Brian had a boost of courage and just went for it all in one shot after that.

"Listen Crush, I can't do this anymore. I think you are so beautiful. I have been waiting for this moment for weeks. I really am interested in getting to know you better and hope we can become closer. I mean...like MORE closer, ya know. I haven't been around many Black girls in my town and the ones that are there, are ugly...I mean...umm."

Crush smiled and began to blush herself. She put her head down just a little and looked away as a shy girl would do. and in a split second she replied.

"That's funny Brian, 'Cause I was wondering when you was gonna say something. Do you know how hard it was for me to find out your schedule so I can finally be in the same room with you? I pulled some strings and found out that you were going to be here at the library today."

"Wow...seriously? You are interested in me?"

"Yeah Brian, look around. How many of us are around here at the Estate. Black folk don't come around these parts here" Crush said imitating a runaway slave voice.

"Oh My God! You're are so funny Crush."

"You should see me do my Salt and Pepa raps."

"Oh My God. I heard some guys from New York City called Run DMC are so cool and this guy I heard the other day too, LL Cool J?"

Brain and Crush sat and talked for hours. When it was time for her to return, Brain walked Crush to her room. On their way, he realized that Crush had a room that was different than any other students there at the Estate. He didn't even realize that he never saw this part of the Campus, ever. As they stood outside her room door, Brian was in awe at the sight of the hallway. This was a beautiful building. So private, that he asked if he would get in trouble being in this building. Crush began to answer when...

"And who is this young man?"

"Dr. Korvach. Hi." Crush answered with a big smile on her face as she gave him a hug.

"Hello Crush. You know this a quite a surprise to have an unexpected guest here at the house. You know the rules Crush. No guest unless I approve it."

"Yes I know. But this is Brian. We known each other for a while now and I asked him to walk me to my room. So it's my fault Dr. Korvach. Please don't be mad at him."

Crush put her puppy dog eyes look on her face and smiled at Dr. Korvach. He looked at Brian and let out a soft sigh.

"Ok Crush. This one time I will allow you to have company here at the house but next time you must let me know when you plan on having guest. Brian you can stay if you would like."

Brian was a little nervous because many of the patients never ever get to really see Dr. Korvach's private life style after their sessions are over. So this was a great honor to him.

"Yes Mr. Dr. Korvach. I would love to stay. I'm very honored to be invited and ...."

While Brian was in the middle of his sentence, Korvach began to walk away without even hearing him finish his statement. The energy was shifted to an uncomfortable feeling in the air. Brain looked at Crush with a puzzled look in his eyes. Crush looked at Korvach walk away as if he really didn't want Brian to stay, but did it for her. Crush opened her door and pulled Brian by his hand inside and closed the door behind him. Inside her room, Brian was even more amazed. Crush's room was not the size of your average room at all. This shit was fucking laced out with all types of modern shit that hadn't even been invented yet in his eyes. He never saw a TV screen the size of a whole wall. The floor was red oak wood. The furniture was all leather and the ceilings were as high as the biggest cathedral Church. Her bed was at the end of the room facing the windows that took the place of the wall that should have been there. The windows faced a meadow field that stretched as far as one acres long leading into the forest at the back of the Estates property. No one ever saw this part of the campus. Her room was so big, she had a section with a dining table that sat twelve people with large candles on each end and one plate set at the end where Crush obviously ate alone. The music system was built into the wall. Her closets were not even visible until she pushed on the wall and it opened up. Brain was so fucking confused, all he could do was whisper to himself. "What the Fuck?" He watched Crush act as if it was normal for a patient to have such special living quarters. Crush seemed so happy to have a guest in her room, especially a boy at that. She continued to move a few things around while making her way to her bed. Brian stood completely still looking around and wondering what the hell was going on, and who the fuck was this girl.

"You can come over here Brian. Don't get all scared now." Her room was so big that her voice actually echoed. Brian snapped out of his thought.

"Sure. Cool. Ok."

He began to walk over to the area where her bed was and looked at pictures of her parents and the Dairy farm as he passed her dressers. He began to put the pieces together. His family had money, but nothing close to what Crush's parents had. He realized that as he was looking at the pictures, he was still walking towards her bed. The room seemed to never end. Finally reaching the bed, his eyes popped out of his head as he looked at a bed never seen before ever. The bed is called an "Extreme Ultra King bed. Measured at an astonishing 12 feet wide by 10 feet long. The king of all king size beds. Eight people can snuggle comfortably and not lose a bit of sleep.

"Ok Crush. I don't know what to say at this point but...who the hell are you?"

Crush fell on her bed laughing real hard, holding her stomach still laughing, she rolled over on her side looking at Brian with a smile.

"You are so funny Brian. Yes. I have been here for a while now. I have a rare condition that Dr. Korvach has been studying since I was about six years old. My condition has been the base for receiving large financial Government Grants to help Dr. Korvach find a cure for my rare condition. So I guess you can say...I'm the poster child for this Estate. So, yes I have special treatment Brian. So, now you don't like me anymore?"

"No I didn't say that. It's just a lot to take in, so suddenly. I was not expecting all of this. Ok! I was not expecting this shit at all but I think I can get use to it. A beautiful girlfriend with a lot of money and a bed room the size of a church...oops! Did I say...girlfriend?"

Crush looked at Brian with a funny look on her face.

"Girlfriend already? Wow! That was fast. We haven't even kissed yet. How do I know if I even want to be your girlfriend, when I haven't tried the goods?"

Brian sat on the bed next to her and leaned over her putting his face one inch shy away from actually touching.

"Well then I guess I have to pass the test then." He placed his lips on hers ever so softly and began to intertwine their tongues. He grabbed her waist and tried not to put his hand up her shirt to grab her breast. But Crush had other plans. She pulled his hand up her shirt and forced him to grab it anyway. Her nipples were so soft. Her skin was as smooth as he could have imagined. She pulled him fully on the bed and on top of her. He couldn't believe how aggressive she was but didn't stop her at all. Crush moaned and groaned as they rubbed up on each other dry humping with very hard sexual pumps. Brian began to get a serious erection while the excitement drove her crazy. Crush wanted him so bad. She was a virgin but had been locked up for so long that she was ready to just get her cherry popped right then, right there, right now.

As they began ravishing each other with force, Brain's eyes spotted something strange up in one corner of the ceiling. He noticed a little black bubble with a red lighted dot inside. He stopped pulling her clothes off and sat up quickly. Crush was confused.

"What's wrong Brian? Why are you stopping? Oh, we need protection? Like a condom?"

"No Crush." Brian said trying not to look directly up at the camera.

"Umm...Don't look. But there's a camera watching us right now."

"What?" Crush whispered as she pulled her shirt down slowly trying not to look obvious.

"Yes. I just noticed it now."

Crush and Brian sat with their backs towards the camera just holding hands and kept the movements at minimal. They began to chuckle at each other.

"Oh My God, Brian, I never really noticed that there was any cameras in here."

"Damn Crush! Why would there be cameras in here anyway?"

"I don't know. That's a damn good question that I will ask Dr. Korvach when you leave."

"Ok...Maybe it's time for me to go anyway. I have to get back to my evening session."

" Ok...I will walk you to the door then."

Walking hand in hand towards the door, Crush told Brian that she had a wonderful day with him. Brian replied the same back. Brian went to give Crush a kiss, when she pulled back shy from maybe being caught on camera. They both laughed and said their goodbyes as he exited Crush's room.

Walking halfway down the hall with a smile on his face, the silence was thick. Brian's mind was racing with the thoughts of how nice it would have been to make love to Crush for the first time. Getting closer to the exit doors leading down the middle wing of the building, there were two corners to turn in either direction left or right. One leading south down another long hallway, and the other left before reaching the exit. Brian was startled by Kenneth turning the corner before reaching the exit. They both paused. Kenneth's piercing eyes gave Brian a chill as he stood there quiet in his grey pin stripped suit, and his custom tailor made lab coat that came down ankle length.

"Brian. May I have a word with you?"
"Sh...sure Dr. Korvach."
"Follow me to my office please."

As they walked down the south wing, Kenneth placed his hand on Brian's shoulder with a semi tight grip leading him down the hall like a police officer would do to a perp making sure he wouldn't try to run. Brian was getting more and more nervous every step towards Dr. Korvach's office. It seemed like the hallway would never end. Finally, coming to a large oak wood door with gold handles, Kenneth released Brian and pulled out his office keys and opened the door. Once again Brian found himself entering a huge room with Victorian leather couches everywhere. Kenneth's Office had only one large double French door and a window opposite of his large Mahogany wooden desk with Lion heads carved in on each corner. The room had a real gloomy feel to it with large lamps that had dim lighting. The kind of room you see in one of those old Vincent Price horror films, the mad scientist's room with all kinds of artifacts, relics, very expensive and priceless paintings covering the walls and books with cobwebs on them. But Kenneth was clean and modern. Although Brian did not believe in Ghost, he could have sworn he heard faded whispers of echoing voices throughout the office. Brain paused and stood there looking in all direction wondering what the fuck was about to happen.

"Brian have a seat. I want to talk to you about this relationship you think you have with Crush Onyx."

Brian really became nervous after hearing Kenneth say that. He knew Kenneth had to be the one watching them interact sexually on

Crush's bed in her room through the camera planted on the ceiling. Brian tried to explain.

"Dr. Korvach...I-I..."
"I said have a seat Brian!"
"Yes sir."

Looking at Dr. Korvach, as he opened the curtains to his window to let some light in, Brian felt like he was going to toss up his lunch from all the anxiety he was feeling. Kenneth sat down in his big leather desk chair, interlocked his fingers and placed them down on his desk, slowly.

"Brian, let me explain something to you about Ms. Crush Onyx. She is like a daughter to me. Basically, I have been raising her since the age of six. I spent so much time with her trying to develop a trusting relationship and bond. If I felt in the slightest way, that someone would ever try to compromise all my work, time, and energy....well, I just don't know how I would react. Sure I would be upset. But you understand what I'm saying Brian? Don't you?"

Brian's answer was all in his face. He didn't have to answer out loud. Kenneth saw in the boy's eyes that he understood quite well what he was trying to get across. Then something strange happened. Brain had shifted the mood from being uncomfortable, to being curious. All the time he did spend with his father coming from a long family history of lawyers, Brian immediately went into defense zone and had a few questions of his own.

"I do understand Dr. Korvach. But I thought this was a facility geared for helping individuals with depression and mental health issues? This isn't a psychiatric ward, is it? I only ask because...let's keep it open and honest Dr., why the cameras? I'm sure my father didn't sign me up to be monitored or medicated."

Kenneth leaned back in his chair and put a very serious face on.

"That is very true Brian. I'm very impressed with your question, and I will assure you that you are not under any type of observation what so ever. There are no cameras in your room but Onyx is a very unique and special case study for this medical practice, and is a very delicate and sensitive matter at hand."

"Onyx?" Brian said leaning forward in his seat tilting his head to the right puzzled.

"Yes Brian. Crush is very.....
Brian cut Dr. Korvach short in his sentence.
"No...you said Onyx? That's her last name isn't it? It almost sounds as if you were referring to someone totally different?"

Now Brian was pushing it being cocky and arrogant in his voice patterns. Dr. Korvach was not pleased with his condescending tone. Korvach leaned forward and stared into Brian's eyes and paused in silence for a few seconds. He stood up and began to walk over towards his mini bar located a few feet away from his desk. He pulled out two plastic cold bottles of spring water. Grabbing two glasses and put ice in them from the ice bucket inside. Walking back, Korvach pointed at the library against his wall taking off his glasses and placing them on his desk.

"Brian what do you know about split personalities? You know, someone creating a whole new person in their heads, actually believing that there's more than one person inside of them living two different lives. The name for this diagnosis is called multiple personality disorder. In both systems of terminology, the diagnosis requires that at least two personalities routinely take control of the individual's behavior with an associated memory loss that goes beyond normal forgetfulness. In addition, symptoms cannot be the temporary effects of drug use or a general medical condition. It's a condition in which a person displays multiple distinct identities or personalities known as alter egos or alters. Each with its own pattern of perceiving and interacting with the environment."

Brian's face completely changed up real quick. He knew that this conversation was going to be something totally unexpected. He wondered what new secret was about to be told to him about that sexy ass girl he was falling for and if she had a condition that would change his perception of her.

"I want you to get that book on the forth high shelf that says Sigmund's Theory on the psyche. You have to grab that ladder and climb a little son. I will pour us some water while you are a good gentlemen and getting that book for me to share some info on our Crush. I feel we got off to a bad start. Let's be open and honest from here on."

Brain shook his head up and down with a silent yes gesture. Walking over to get the ladder with his back now turned in Korvach's direction, Korvach opened his desk drawer and secretly pulled out a small bottle with hand written letters in black ink on a white label that read, TEST SERUM MC2. He wasn't sure how much to administer being it was in its test phase, so he put five drops in just to be careful. He had been working on a mind control serum for years. Science seems to have a way of making mankind want more than it has to offer. Pushing it to the furthest brink, Korvach was successful in going undetected by Brian. He sat back and waited for Brian to bring the book back to his desk.

Brian handed Korvach the book and sat back down in the plush couch, but not before grabbing the cold glass of water that was placed there for him. Sipping on the water slowly, Korvach began speaking again.

"Sigmund Freud was the best Neurologist known in that Century. He made incredible break throughs dealing with mental science. He discovered that the human brain is the most powerful organism on this planet. And is also recorded that the human brain is the center of the human nervous system enclosed in the cranium. It has the same general structure as the brains of other mammals, but is over three times as large as the brain of a typical mammal with an equivalent body size. Most of the expansion comes from the cerebral cortex, a convoluted layer of neural tissue that covers the surface of the forebrain. Especially expanded are the frontal lobes, which are associated with executive functions such as self-control, planning, reasoning, and abstract thought. That's why we are at the top of the food chain not because we have strength or size. There are many larger mammals on this planet that can overpower us with ease. The killer whale can weigh up to 10 tons and breathe in and out of water. We on the other hand will drown and definitely can't measure up against its strength."

Korvach kept rambling on as much as he could, waiting for the serum to kick in. But nothing was happening out of the unordinary with Brian's reactions. In fact, Brian seemed to be getting bored with Brain Talk 101. This went on for about a half hour.

"Dr. Korvach. I don't mean to cut you off but I know most of this information already. So why are we really here in your office? What are you going to tell me about Crush?"

"Well Brian. How do you really feel about Crush?"

Brain paused.

"I'm becoming a man now Dr. Korvach. I have feelings for Crush that I never felt before. Sure I had my fun in High School. I had many cheer leaders giving me sex anytime I wanted. I was the star player on my basketball team. That came with the title. But there's something different about Crush. I feel like she can be the one. You know, like my parents in college. That's when they fell in love. But....anyway....I just like her very much. But what's......."

Brian began to let out a batch of soft coughs repeatedly for a few seconds.

"Excuse me...Umm..like I was saying. What's going on with Crush? Why do you have her room full of cameras? What's so special about her?"

"Well Brian. Crush was born with a split personality. An alter ego per say. She has two people inside her. The one you are falling for is Crush. The one you haven't met is Onyx. Yes, we had to distinguish them separately by name in or order for her to continue developing with knowledge of which one she was, and who she was at that time of an episode. You have no idea what you are getting involved in. Would you like to know who Onyx is? I can arrange that for you Brian. I'm sure you would be most surprised and probably taken by her too. She is quite the party girl. Crush is more reserved. Onyx is...well....different."

Brian sat back and sunk himself inside the couches back pillow. He kept rubbing the top of his head making weird faces as if he was confused. Korvach stood up and walked over to the window. He gazed out onto the meadows as it was nearing late evening. The wind began to pick up speed, blowing leaves around on the lawn two flights down. The clouds started filling with the color of grey, as if a rain storm was brewing to soon lay down its wrath of heavy rain. He pushed his lab coat to the side and pulled out a pipe from the inside of his jacket. With the clouds getting darker and darker, and the wind continuously picking up speed, Brian started to feel a little dizzy sitting in his spot. Finally the weather gave in to the first cracking of thunder. The lightning followed with a loud bang. Dr. Korvach still looking out the window took his gold lighter out of the jacket pocket and lit the tobacco. Then the second sighting of a thick burst of lightning flashed brighter through the window. Again, the loud sound of a bang. This time it was followed by a slight rattle that moved just the top of the water in the glasses. The sweet smell of cherry scent tobacco and smoke started to consume the gloomy area surrounding Dr. Korvach. He turned around and asked Brian if he was alright. The darker it got outside his window, the darker the area got where Korvach was standing. It seemed as if he was slowly fading into the curtains after every puff on his pipe. Brian began to rub both his eyes as he tried to speak but the only thing that came out were soft mumbles.

"Dr...D...D...Dr.   Korvach...I..I...Don't   feel   so...good. W...w...what's...hap-happening to me?"

Brian's eyes became foggy and blurred as he tried to sit himself up. Between each blink, he could see the figure of Dr. Korvach moving closer and closer. His attempt to sit up was a failure. He fell back into the couches pillows unable to pull himself up. The voice, the voice sounded distant and faded. "Brriiaann......Arrreeeee...youuu ookkk...." He continued to rub his eyes as they began to water. He could still feel himself fading slowly. He could not control his movements at all. He felt Dr. Korvach opening his eyelids and shining a light into them calling his name. But the voice was fading further and further away.

Dr. Korvach stood over Brian's limp body as he took another toke on his pipe. The sound of heavy rain beat against the French door windows hard and loud. Kenneth walked over to close the curtains for more privacy. Sitting back down at his desk, he reached back into the draw and took out the serum again and gazed at the bottle. He looked back up at Brian slouched down in the seat...

"Brian, I will count to five and my voice only will be the voice that you listen to. I am Dr. Kenneth Korvach. You will listen and follow my every order after I'm finish counting to five. Is that understood Brian?"

"Yesssss." Brain answered in a low soft hypnotic tone. Korvach began counting.

"1, -2, -3, -4, - 5. Brain stand up and walk over here to me."

Without a second of hesitation, as if Brian was still in a cheerful teenage mood, he went over to Korvach and asked him "what?" with a big smile on his face. Kenneth was amazed. He began to say something, when Crush was knocking at the locked door outside his office. Her voice was muffled just a little behind the doors.

"Kenneth? Kenneth? I need to talk to you? Kenneth I hear you in there!" Crush knocked harder and faster. "Come on Kenneth! I really need to talk to you. You know I will sit out here all night until you open the door." Crush said in a sweet girly voice as if she was talking to her own father playing outside his door.

Dr. Korvach stood up and took a puff from his pipe staring at the door with a sinister look.

"I'm coming Crush. Give a minute."

Korvach opened the draw on the right side of the desk. This time he pulled out yet another clear transparent medicine bottle with a white paper label. This one had the writing…Inhibitor 67. He grabbed a syringe needle and placed both of them in his lab coat pocket.

"I'm coming right now sweetie."

The thunder was loud and hard rain beat against the window pane as he walked over to the door. Crush was playful as she entered the room looking at Dr. Korvach. Until she looked across the room in the direction of his desk.

"What is Brian doing here?"
"He's here for you Crush."

Crush began to walk slowly over towards Brian with her arms folded and crossed over each other on her chest. Meanwhile, with her back turned, Korvach was filling the syringe with the serum Inhibitor 67. As she got closer, she was confused as to why every time she called Brian's name, he stood there with his back turned looking into space with this silly smile on his face.

"Brian?...Brian?...what the hell is wrong with Brian, Kenneth? Why is he smiling like that?"
Crush shook Brian and still nothing. Not paying any attention to Kenneth, she turned her head around and Dr. Korvach was fast to inject her neck with the serum from the syringe. Crush pushed Kenneth's hand away with force while backing away in confusion.

"WHAT THE FUCK!"

Crush's eyes became heavy with each blink. Falling forward into Kenneth's arms, she tried to speak.

"What......are....yo.."

"Now now Crush. It will be ok. Just relax my darling. Just relax."

Picking Crush up and softly placing her limp body on the couch, Kenneth told Brian to sit beside Crush. Brian obeyed and sat next to Crush with the silly smile still on his face. Kenneth sat back in his seat at his desk, took a sip of water and waited.

"Thank you....Damn it took you fucking forever. I told you how fucking bored I get being locked up in that fucking cramped up room in this bitches head!"

"Now Onyx, be nice. I told you about your language. I don't like to hear you talk like that in my office."

"Oh fucking stop it Kenneth. Save that bullshit for Miss Prissy Ass Crush. Besides, you like it when I talk that shit when we fuck! Speaking of fucking....who's the nerd? He's cute too...OHHH...you want to have a threesome?"

Crush no more. ONYX was out and ready to behave in the manner of her true birth nature. Onyx was in every way not shy. She was bold with her words. Bold in her behavior. Bold enough even to murder and kill with no remorse. This personality was the most deadly in every way.

"No Onyx. I have some new tests that I want you to be a part of. As you can see, he is under my complete control and for what I have planned, I need both of you to interact and get to know each other."

Onyx stood up and began to pace back and forth while loosening up her hair, letting it fall back down to her back. Kenneth on the other hand was watching Onyx closely. Knowing how she can be, he didn't want to take a chance on her doing something crazy. So he stood up and walked over to his library and pulled a book from off the shelf. He opened the book, only knowing, it was not just a book. It had been custom made with pages cut from the center. It was designed to hold small items inside it. He had a small spray bottle with an airborne Inhibitor Serum #68, that he can spray in Onyx's face that would paralyze her for a few minutes just so he can use the syringe with Inhibitor 67 to send her back to the far locked away room of Crush's psyche, if necessary. He kept it in his hand at all times during any time with Onyx.

"Ok, so what's the deal with nerdo then? How do I fit in this test thing you're talking about Kenny?"

Dr. Korvach told Onyx to sit next to Brian. She squinted her eyes at Korvach while sitting down beside Brian. She placed her hand on his crotch area feeling his dick. She began to unzip his pants. "Onyx! STOP THAT!" he yelled. He went back to his desk and pulled out a big yellow

envelope. "Here's what I want you to do."

CHAPTER TWELVE:

"*All That Does Happen*"

"I can't believe what the fuck just happen!...Care to explain that shit Karen?"

"I'm...I'm...not sure Tom?" Dr. Karen Sanchez said with her hands shaking by her side.

Crush began to sit up off the couch still shaking her head at what just happened herself. She sat there for a few more seconds just staring around the room, breathing in deep breaths then letting them out slowly. One hand placed on her chest as she then focused her eyes on Karen.

"Crush, are you ok?" Dr. Karen asked as she walked over to Crush with a slight limp in her walk from the hard push and putting her hand on her shoulder.

"I don't know what to think right about now Karen. I just can't...can't figure out what's happening to me? This wasn't expected at all. It was like she...she...she took complete control over...."

"Over what? What the hell is going on in this session Dr. Sanchez!" Dr. Thomas Thorp said while stomping his feet real hard on the floor looking at them both.

"Let me explain Karen. Well Dr. Thomas, I'm not sure if you know who I am. But I have a rare mental disorder. I was born with a split personality. Or shall I say an Alter Ego that is completely untamable. She is one of the worst things that ever happen to society. She is the Daughter of Satan I tell you. She's killed so many people, and I had no knowledge of it for many years. Finding out that I was a sick experiment that Dr. Kenneth Korvach had created, there are some things that have now come back to haunt me. Somehow Onyx, the other half, has found ways to break free from the psyche part of my mind that Kenneth had placed her in. I'm still not sure what he did to her when I was under whatever confinement he had me in while he let her free. It's so much to explain. Just let me catch my breath please."

Dr. Thomas and Karen paused for a few seconds. Thomas turned to Karen and shook his head at her in a manner that silently said, she knows better to try some dumb shit like that without proper assistance. Karen put her head down and walked over to a pillow that was tossed on the floor when Onyx had her in her grasp. Thomas then turned to Crush and walked over to Karen's work desk were she had a few glasses and a pitcher of cold water. He filled up a glass and sat down beside Crush handing her the water.

"Now I really need to hear more about this disorder Ms. Crush. It seems you are going to need more than one Doctor to help you deal with this rare case."

He said turning his head in Karen's direction with his eyes squinting at her through his glasses.

Crush grabbed the glass slowly from his hand with a small smile on her face; she took a sip, crossed her legs, took a deep breath, and then let out a soft sigh. Karen placed the pillow back on the leather couch behind Crush's back so she can get more comfortable to continue. She then sat in a chair completely opposite of her and Dr. Thorp.

999

The man's head hit each step with a loud thumping sound as Leto dragged his body down the staircase and into the room her and her sister Asteria called, "The Room of Truth." Leto whistled and hummed a tone all the way down. Reaching the basement, she continued to pull his lifeless body with ease to a wall with a washing machine and dryer placed against it. She pushed a few buttons on the washer's digital display keypad and in seconds, the wall did a complete half turn exposing an entrance to the room. She pulled him inside and shouted "lights on!" The room lit up instantly. The room was filled with all kinds of different tables with custom designed torturing device attachments. One made with black leather ankle and hand straps, and a head and neck placement leather leash strap. Most of them look like something a dominatrix would use during her sexual punishment sessions with a sick and perverted client.

Leto tapped on her bottom lip with her finger tip as she stood there trying to decide which one to use. She smiled and looked up towards the ceiling and said out loud, "YES!" and grabbed his leg and positioned him belly down on the floor. Moments later he was completely ass naked, hanging mid level in the middle of room with his ankles in leather straps buckled tightly around them. His arms hung loosely almost scraping the floors surface as his body spun slowing in rotation. His wrists were handcuffed, and his mouth was duct taped. Leto popped open a little pill and waved it under his nose back and forth until his eyes opened and he began to breath heavy through his nose as his vision became clearer. Leto whistled as she sharpened a small carving knife. She pulled up a chair, sat in it, spread her legs with her crotch directly in view of the man's face while his body continued to spin in slow rotation. The sweat was thick on his forehead.

"Now, you already know the drill. So why die trying to protect the name of the person who sent you straight to your painful and slow death? Oh... you are going to go through some shit in a few minutes that will seem like a lifetime."

Leto spun him completely around facing her until he was still.

"So, to show you I won't waste time asking over and over again, I'm just going to start carving until you scream their name."

Leto stood up and did just that. She took the sharp carving knife and began cutting and pealing the top layer of his skin from the shoulder down. The man's screams were muffled because of the duct tape that covered his mouth tightly.

"I can't hear you? You said what?...As the Blood came pouring down in big globs hitting the floor, she began carving the flesh off his other arm down to the wrist. His eyes rolled back in his head as the pain caused his body to jilt and jerk back and forth.

"Oh shit, my bad." As she giggled to herself watching him suffer. "Damn. I forgot your mouth was taped up yo." She removed the tape pulling it so hard it nearly ripped his skin off his upper lip. Before the hit man could catch his breath, Leto started to carve the skin around his balls off. His screams were loud and echoed. Sick and twisted, Leto dropped the huge chunk of flesh on the floor and placed the tip of the knife inside the hole on the tip of his dick.

"OK...OK! I WILL TELL YOU...PLEASE DON'T DO ME LIKE THIS...PLEASE...PLEASE!" He shouted with tears running down his forehead.

"Ok, it was Pretty face! He ordered us to kill you. And the serum your sister has is not to bring Onyx back, but to poison Crush and kill her and take over the Sandbox!"

"Wow, you said some deep shit there yo. So where is Pretty face now?"

He paused to long. Leto started to carve the flesh off his left thigh up to his ankle. His screams were loud and filled with much pain. Blood gushed everywhere splattering all over Leto's face as she took pleasure in watching him suffer more and more. She backed away with a grin looking down at him. She giggled with joy.

"OK...OK...HE KNOWS ASTERIA IS ON HER WAY TO KILL HIM NOW! HE SET A TRAP FOR HER AT HIS PLACE! He begins to let out a soft snickering laugh as blood continues to pour down his carved up limbs.

"FUCK YOU BITCH! I know I'm a dead man anyway. But I hope he lets all his team take turns on her ass, raping her and fucking that little pretty pussy until it bleeds." He continues to laugh even harder as his body spins slowly upside down.

Leto steps back. This time she was not smiling. She looked him dead in his eyes before she grunted and walked off returning with a chainsaw. She pulled the cord, and the loud sound of its chains grinding echoed through the room as she began to chop, chop, and chop his limbs until pieces were everywhere. She took a deep breath, looked up and her eye filled with water. She dropped the chainsaw and ran out the room quickly to the nearest phone. She picked up the phone and dialed Asteria's cell phone frantically.

999

Agents Candice and Michelle sit in their GMC truck across the street from Crush's condo complex scoping the entrance. They sit there quietly sipping on soda. Candice has her hands on the steering wheel looking up through the windshield in the direction of Crush's balcony. Michelle sighs and turns in her direction.

"What the fuck are we waiting for Candice? Let's just go and bug the condo and get the hell out before she comes home."

"Yeah I know. But we have to be real careful on this. Remember, if she happens to come in, how do we explain why we are in her house planting bugs and cameras."

"Well, The longer we sit here she just might walk in." Michelle says sarcastically and rolls her eyes looking back out the passenger's window.

Candice stares at Michelle and smiles. They both laugh and open their doors and step out. They both pull their jackets over their guns while Michelle grabs a black duffle bag full of all the equipment they need to plant in Crush's condo. Locking the door, they jog across the street through passing cars. Reaching the building's lobby, they walk through unnoticed making their way to the elevator. Lucky there wasn't anyone getting on the same elevator, Michelle reaches into her jacket pocket she grabs a small black device that looks like a car alarm hand switch. She presses the red button disabling the camera for a few seconds. Just enough time for Candice to stick her universal special F.B.I. key in the slot that will take them straight to Crush's floor. Getting off the elevator, the hallway was quite. They tip toed to Crush's double doors and kneeled down to open the duffle bag and pull out the lock picking equipment. Some doors the universal key does not work on. So they had to go old school.

Pushing the doors open slowly, with their guns drawn, they walked in with their backs sliding against the left side wall. It was as quite as a church during confession time. They closed the door shut and made their way inside a little further.

"Do you see this shit Candice? This bitch's house looks like something straight on the rich and famous cribs."

"Yea, this place is very nice Michelle."

"Oh My God. Look at this kitchen." Michelle said as she walked in the kitchen to the right, and Candice made her way down into the sunken living room area.

They both began to pull out all the equipment out the bags and start bugging every phone near them in the living room and kitchen areas. Michelle grabbed a stepping stool and started to unscrew the light fixture to put a hidden camera inside. Candice was making her way around the living room doing the same.

"So Michelle, what do you think we should do about this Brian character?" Candice said as she was laying on her back on the wooden oak wood floor planting a bug under Crush's antique coffee table.

"I say we just let Crush do her, and he will come to us later. Right now we have to see how all this shit is going to help us catch Onyx, when Onyx isn't even here anymore. Honestly Candice, I'm not feeling this is a good idea as much as I did before. That information we got doesn't sound good. This is weird and creeping me out even more now."

"Michelle Blake! You getting soft now? Not the baddest female F.B.I. agent of this generation. Miss Jada Pinket Smith has nothing on me...yo yo yo...I'm a bad bitch yo."

Candice started to laugh as Michelle stuck her middle finger up in her direction. They both chuckled as Candice got up and headed towards the back area. Michelle was still putting cameras all throughout the kitchen area, when she thought she heard the front door close quietly. She slowly and silently, in a slow motion pace stepped down off the ladder. Before she could reach for her fire arm, she was staring down the barrel of a big desert eagle had gun. The man holding the gun pointed at her face signaled her to be quiet and move back slowly. He silently pointed at her gun and signaled with a hand gesture for her to place it on the floor and back away. Michelle did what he said. She put down her gun and backed away. They both stared silently at each other for a few seconds when the sound of a guns hammer cocked back.

"Slowly put that gun down and place your hands in the air sir!"

Candice was about 30 feet away in the middle of Crush's hallway that lead to the back rooms pointing her gun at the man. The man continued to point his gun at Michelle.

"Sorry miss, but that's not going to happen. You two broke into the wrong condo apartment and I will blow her head clear off before you let off a shot. So you drop your gun. Or it's going to get real ugly up in here in a few seconds."

"We are the F.B.I. And we have a warrant for the woman who resides at this address. So I will ask you one more time to place your gun down and back away from her. If you shoot an FBI agent and live, your life will get a lot more complicated sir. So you don't want to do anything drastic."

The situation was thick. Candice knew they were in deep shit now. So why not lie anyway. The man refused to put his gun down. Then he pointed the gun even closer to Michelle's Face.

"Ok sir! Listen, I'm going to put my gun down slowly and reach for my badge. So you don't have to feel threatened. We are here for Ms. Crush Onyx. What you think you know about this woman, or what she has told you is False. She is a very dangerous woman. She is wanted in three different countries for murder. We don't want to bring you into this, but what you're doing is only going to get you deep in a world of shit."

Candice put her gun down pointed at the floor. They both looked at each other for a few seconds.

"Too late. I'm already in too deep. Plus I know who she is Miss F.B.I. agent. She's been my Girlfriend since we were teenagers. You must be talking about Onyx. Not Crush. So what makes you think I'm going to let you take her again Agents Candice Sums and Michelle Blake? It's been what, Five years now?"

In a split second, Michelle pushed the gun away and jumped clear over the kitchen counter knocking all the appliances over as she dived onto the living room floor and rolled behind the couch. The man darted across the room behind the kitchen table, turning it over for cover as he let off a full clip in Candice's direction. Candice hit the floor as bullets shattered the wall sending chunks of white plastered sheetrock dropping on her head as she covered it blinded by all the dust. In seconds, the man reloaded his clip and started shooting at the couch were Michelle was crouched down cocking her gun. After a few bullets pierced the leather fabric also missing her by inches, she returned fire. Candice did the same. Bullets were flying everywhere throughout Crush's condo. For a few more seconds as they all were reloading their guns, Candice screamed out at the man.

"Brian Century! We know who you are! And you just signed your death warrant you son of a bitch!"

The room was still. Michelle and Candice waited for a response from Brian. But he said nothing back. Michelle peeked over the couch real fast and then put her head back down.

"Brian...give it up Bro! We will shoot you dead man! So why don't we just do this the easy way! At least you live Brother! I don't want to kill you!" Michelle screamed out.

Still no response. They both slowly got up from the floor and looked in the direction of the kitchen table. They both looked as the curtains from the balcony door flapped in the wind. They realized Brian made a quiet escape off the balcony without them even noticing. Michelle looked at Candice putting her gun down.

"This is some Bullshit yo!"

999

Crush took another sip of water and leaned back on the couch. Dr. Karen and Dr. Thomas were in awe after Crush had told them all about her life and what she knew about Dr. Kenneth Korvach. She sat there silently and took another sip of water. Dr. Thomas started rubbing his bald scalp shaking his head back and forth.

"Well Ms. Crush, that is amazing. The medical breakthrough that Korvach has achieved will make history. How many people know of what you just told us?" Thomas asked as he got up and started pacing back and forth across the office smiling real hard.

"No one but me. I'm just finding out about new things myself. As I'm finding out all new things, I'm just as amazed as you. It's going to be a long and hard road for me now. I need help. I can't do it by myself Doctors."

"It's going to be alright Crush. We are here to help you get through this." Karen said as she looked at Crush with water in her eyes.

Dr. Thomas was still pacing back and forth tapping a pen against his glasses. He then rushed to Karen's desk grabbing a yellow writing memo pad and started writing real fast on it mumbling to himself. Karen asked Crush if she was ok to go home, and she would walk her to the elevator while Dr. Thorp was going through his amazed phase and writing notes of what just happened. Crush grabbed her things and both her and Karen walked out of the office. Karen kept her arm around Crush's shoulder showing her a little comfort while they waited for the elevator to arrive. Crush told Karen it was ok, and she was just fine, and for her to go back to her office and call her later so they can set up her next appointment. Karen gave Crush a big hug and walked away as the elevator doors opened up. Crush waved goodbye with a girly smile on her face and entered the elevator.

Crush leaned up against the elevator wall with her arms folded one over the other. There was a handsome young Doctor in the elevator talking on his cell phone. Just them two were alone for the ride down six fights. It was very late in the evening by the time the session was over. The hospital was quiet. The late night shift had turned over. 5th floor. The elevator doors opened up. No one enters. Crush turns in his direction and smiled at the handsome young Doctor. He smiles back, as he continued to talk on his cell phone. The doors close. 4th floor. Elevator doors open. No one gets on. Crush continues to smile even harder at the handsome Doctor. He smiles back even harder as well. He tells the person on the other line that he will call them back. The elevator door closes. 3rd floor. The doors open. No one enters. The handsome Doctor is shaking Crush's hand introducing himself to her. She tells him her name. The doors close. 2nd floor. The elevator doors open. No one gets on. Crush has the young handsome Doctor pressed up against the elevator wall locking lips as they kiss each other with raw passion. The doors close. 1st floor. The elevator doors open. Crush gets off alone. As she is walking through the Hospital lobby, making her way past a few nurses, she smiles at one of them and waves good bye. She pulls the clip from her hair letting it drop down to the center of her back. The automatic exit doors open while she walks through them onto the City Street. The air is crisp. The New York City sounds create music that only a real City person could enjoy. She reaches into her pocket. Pulling out a cell phone. She dials out. They answer.

"Yeah, it's me.....I'M BACK!

Coming Soon

By

Geoffrey McClanahan

The Epic Psychological Thriller Trilogy Collection
Parts 2 & 3

"CRUSH ONYX2"...Onyx Unleashed...

"CRUSH ONYX3"...There can only be one...

EliteRoyalties LLC Publications